To Charisse our favorite
Neighbor. Wes

1

ROMANCE ON THE BEACH

A NOVELETTE

BY

WB CARTER

July 5, 2024

The characters and the incidents are the product of the author's imagination and are unrelated to persons, places, or events.

ACKNOWLEDGMENTS

I WANT TO THANK ALL OF MY EDITORS AS THEY DEVOTED A LOT OF TIME TO REREAD THIS BOOK.

I want to dedicate this book to my wonderful spouse for letting me spend so much time writing it.

I hope you enjoy the book. It contains romance, excitement, danger, and fun.

Ed Martin owns a small real estate office in a small Indiana town. He is 45 and single. Ed is also a member of the Air National Guard, where he is a Col and a pilot. He flies the F4 Phantom Jet on weekends. On a flight, he had an accident, which made him consider retiring. Ed has become bored with his routine and life. He needs a vacation. He spends time with his friends Jim and Bill at a local Golf club and bar. It seems his real estate business is dominating his life. He decides he needs to get away for a while. His friend Bill tells him to visit his beach house in Destin, Florida. Ed accepts, and he goes to Destin, FL, Where he can fish on the beach, play golf, and maybe enjoy some nightlife. When he arrives there, he goes out to play golf and to a couple of nightclubs where he finds attractive friends. He might finally meet someone he would be attracted to. He finds out he loves this place. Ed is a romantic type of guy easy to make friends with until he meets Cindy. Does he become a one-lady man?

It's Saturday morning. Ed gets up, looks out the window, and thinks it's a great day to go flying. He puts on his FLT clothes and heads out to the Guard base where he checks in at Base Ops.

He asks the lieutenant at the flight desk, "Do I have a plane scheduled for this morning?

The Lieutenant replies, "Yes, you do, sir. You are scheduled for a high-speed practice low-level run this morning."

Ed picks up his flight log and heads down to the locker room. The other pilots were there, and one walked over to him.

"Good morning, Ed. I'm your wingman this morning. It looks like we're going over the Great Lakes this morning for our high-speed, low-level run. It should be easy and fun," said Major Scott.

Lt. Andrew walks over to him and says, "I'm your WSO today."

"Great," said Ed.

They picked up their shutes and life preservers and walked out to their planes. The FLT chief was there waiting for Ed.

"Good morning, Col," said Msgt Westerfield. Your plane is ready. He helped Ed get on the plane.

The pilots started their planes and taxed out to the run-up area, where they checked the planes out. Ed called the tower.

Lacon Tower, this is Gator 683, a fleet of two ready for takeoff," Ed said over his radio.

"Gator 683 Cleared for take-off, depart to the north after take-off and contact Indy center on 134.2 passing thru 4,000 ft." said the tower

"Will do." Replied Ed after reading back about his clearance to the tower.

Upon passing through 4,000 ft, Ed called Indy. "Indy approach this id Gator 683 flt of two passing through 4,000 ft."

Indy replied, "Roger Gator 683, you are clear to flt lever 230 direct to dame fix. Proceed then to 2300 altitude to begin your run."

Ed read back the instructions and began climbing to FLT level 230. They maintained the altitude until they reached the fix, cruising at 510 kn.

"Ok, Scott, let's go." Said Ed.

They descended to 2300 ft and leveled out. They pushed their throttles forward and reached their maximum speed. They were cruising along for about ten minutes when Ed heard a loud explosion to his rear. The fire light came on on the right engine.

"Ed, your plane is on fire. You and Andrew get out of there.

Ed reached down and pulled his ejection handles. Ed and Andrew both came flying out of the burning plane. Their chutes opened, and they hit the water almost immediately. Both were safe. Their life preservers opened up. Ed and Andrew were within 30 feet of each other.

A fishing boat was nearby. It had watched the whole ordeal and then headed over to the pilots. "Hey, you guys need a lift," it said. The fisherman helped them into the boat.

Ed and Andrew were both soaking wet and cold. "I'm Charlie; here is some blanket for you. Sit back and I will take you to shore,"

"Thanks," said Ed.

When they arrived at the shore, the police and EMTs were there waiting. Ed and Andrew got a ride to the nearest hospital, where they were checked over and given dry clothing.

A doctor came in to see them. "You gentlemen are in fine shape, and you can go. There is a military vehicle waiting outside for you."

Ed and Andrew left and got into the vehicle. The driver, a SGT, turned and said. I'm taking you to the airport, where a plane is waiting to take you guys home.

"Great." Said Ed. "I guess we will go through a lot of interrogations about the accident,"

"We will." Said Andrew.

Ed and Andrew arrived back at the Guard Base, and a car took them to a briefing room, where the Colonel of accident investigations was waiting for them.

Ed and Andrew left the briefing room and said their goodbyes. Ed went over to his commander's office.

Ed walked in, saluted his Commander, and sat down. He was tired. "Good morning," said Col Anderson. "It sounds like you had a hell of an ordeal. How are you feeling?"

"" I'm fine. I've been thinking my 20 years are up, and I would like to retire. Said Ed.

The Commander said, "Well, Ed, you are a great asset to our program here, but I can understand where you are coming from. I will start your paperwork, and it will be thru by tomorrow; you enjoy your retirement."

Ed left the office, went down, and cleaned out his locker. He went to his car and looked around. I will miss this place. He headed home.

It was Saturday evening. He went to his local hang-out and had a beer and a tenderloin sandwich. He then went home and crashed for the evening. He was really tired.

It's Monday morning, and Ed's alarm goes off. Ed looks at the clock. It's 5:00. He slowly gets up, thinking of another day dealing with clients looking at buying and selling homes. He gets up, gets a cup of coffee, and sits down, thinking that life has become the same old routine. He gets dressed and heads into town to his office, Martins Real Estate. He walks in, says good morning to his staff, enters his office sits down. Mary brings him a cup of coffee. Thanks, Mary. "Your messages are there in your box," said Mary.

He picks up his stack of messages and looks at them. It's time for the daily staff meeting and he takes the messages. His staff comprises his secretary, closing broker, and two associate brokers. He walks in.

"Good morning, everyone." They all return the good mornings. They began discussing the business of the day.

Jim starts the meeting out. Ed, you have two closings today, and your client, the Williams, wants to meet and look at houses. Bill, you have to schedule the Young's house closing. And I have one closing and one showing. We are swamped.

Ed looks at his messages and looks at Jim and Bill.

"You know, I was thinking this morning. For the past few weeks, it seems that I have been more busy and have been getting tired from working all the time. I haven't taken a vacation for over two years." He hands his messages to Jim and Bill. They take them, and they look at Ed.

"I will handle my closings today, and one of you can take the Williams coming in today. Call them and schedule the time," said Ed.

Ed says, "I will take two weeks off; you handle the office. I don't know where I'm going yet, but I must get away for a while."

Bill looks at Ed and says, "You know I have a beach house in Destin. Florida, why don't you go and stay there? It's a nice place, you can fish and relax for a while. Bill and I can handle your work here in the office."

Ed thinks about the offer. He pauses, and his mind reminisces about his time at the Air Force Base in Destine. Those were good times there. He thinks about the times with his buddies at the Bars, playing golf, and the food being great. I loved that place.

Hey Ed, "Did you hear me? I have a place in Destine, and you can go down there and stay as long as you want," Bill said.

Ed said, "I think I will. I want to leave right away. Get me the keys and directions, and I'll leave this afternoon."

He smiles, walks out the door, and heads home to pack. At noon, Bill brought him the keys to his beach house

13

with a package about the area. They talked briefly about the area and how to find the beach house.

Destine is a resort area in the panhandle of Florida. It has an active-duty Air Force Base. Many vacationers come there in the summer to spend time on its large white sandy beaches. There are plenty of places to have a good meal and enjoy the nightlife.

Ed said, "Thanks. Bill. I do need the rest, as it has been a busy year." They shook hands and Bill left.

Ed finished packing, loaded his car, locked his house up, and headed south down I65. He drove for about 3 hours and stopped for gas. The weather was perfect. He drove on until just north of Birmingham and pulled off where he had made reservations at a Hilton Inn. It was almost 7 pm and he was hungry. After checking in, he went to the Cracker Barrel nearby and ordered something to eat.

Ed got up the following day, took his suitcases to the car, returned to the hotel, and ate breakfast there. The sun was shining as he was gassing up his car. He headed down I65 through Birmingham and Montgomery, where he jumped off I65 onto 131 South. He drove on for another 3 hours to Destin. It did not take him long to find Bill's Beach house on the beach. It was a large one-story home on stilts. It was painted a light pinkish green (Beachy Color); it had a large deck on the back with steps going down to the beach. Ed parked his car under the house.

Ed got out of the car and looked around. "Wow, this is nice," he said. He unloaded the car and took everything up to the house. Ed looked around the house and said, "This is great." He unpacked and walked out on the deck. The waves were making a soothing noise.

He went back in and looked in the refrigerator, and there was some Busch beer. "Perfect," he said. He grabbed one, returned to the deck, sat in a chair, and watched the beach and water, enjoying the beer. After about 45 minutes, he decided to get some groceries. I will need some snacks and things to eat while I am here.

After a quick trip to the local Walmart for a week's worth of groceries, Ed took a leisurely drive around the area. He spotted a coffee shop, a couple of bars, and even signs pointing to the local golf course. "This place has everything I need," he thought, feeling reassured. He returned to the house and stowed away his groceries, ready to start his vacation.

As the afternoon sun began to dip, Ed felt a surge of excitement. "I'm going to need some fishing gear," he realized. He set off to the bait shop he had noticed earlier, eager to start a new adventure. After purchasing a fishing pole, a surf fishing rig, and some bait shrimp, he was ready to try his hand at fishing in the ocean.

It was late afternoon, and he was getting hungry. He had seen a small restaurant café down the road. He headed there and went in. A waiter came over, and he ordered a coffee and country-fried steak he had seen on the menu. He sat there for a while and noticed a couple of ladies were there. They were glancing over at him and discussing something. After he finished his dinner, he paid for it. As he left, he walked by them.

"Nice evening, ladies, isn't it," Ed greeted them with a smile. He bid them farewell, got into his car, and drove home. Climbing the stairs to his house, he realized it was getting late. The fatigue from the trip was catching up with him. 'I think I'll just crash for the night,' he thought to himself.

The following day, he opened his eyes and looked out the window. The sun was shining bright. He got up, showered, and dressed for the day. He made himself a cup of coffee, then went to the deck, sat in a chair, and watched the beach where the waves for a while. Several people were walking on the beach. Some were picking up shells.

After he finished his coffee, he picked up his fishing pole. It looked like a good day to go fishing. He rigged his poles, picked up his bait, put on his hat, and picked up his poles and chair.

He strolled to the beach, the sand warm beneath his feet. Baiting his hook, he cast his line into the surf. Placing his pole in a holder, he settled into his chair and donned his sunglasses. The sun's rays warmed his face as he sat there, the rhythmic sound of the waves lulling him into a state of relaxation. His gaze was fixed on his pole when a lady jogged by. Ed's eyes followed her, admiring her beauty. 'She's pretty,' he thought.

She paused and asked him, "Catching anything."

"Nothing yet," he said.

Ed glanced up at her, she had nice brunette hair, a nice smile, and excellent natural lips. She looked perfect in her jogging outfit.

"Are you here on vacation?" she asked.

"Yes, I'm here for some fishing and relaxation, just for a couple of weeks," Ed replied. "Are you from here?" he inquired, curious about her origin.

"No, I'm from Tennessee, down for a couple of weeks for sun and relaxation like you." She spoke.

"Where are you staying." She asked Ed.

"I'm staying in this house of my friend's. How about you?" he asked her.

"I'm staying at the coastline condos down the beach away, "She replied. "I'm Cindy, what's your name?" She asked.

Ed stood up. "I'm Ed," he said and reached out his hand. "Glad to meet you, Cindy."

They smiled at each other, and Cindy said, "I've got to run; maybe we will run into each other again soon."

"That would be good," said Ed. They nodded at each other. Cindy went on jogging down on the beach.

Ed watched her for a few seconds then turned to watch his fishing line. Cindy turned and smiled at him and continued jogging down the beach. Ed was smiling too.

Just then Ed's pole jumped. Ed jumped up, grabbed his fishing pole, and reeled in a nice Pompano. He placed it in his bucket of water, baited his hook, and threw out his line again.

He sat down smiling, thinking about today. It was a good day. He caught another pompano and threw it in his bucket. That's enough fish for me. He picked everything up and went up to the house. He cleaned his fish and put them in the refrigerator.

I think I will head down to the coffee shop for a donut. He parked on the side of the Donut Hole shop. He went in and sat down at a table. A waiter came over, gave him a menu, and asked what he would like to drink; he ordered coffee and two donuts. The waiter left and returned with his coffee and a donut.

Just as he took a sip of his coffee, Cindy walked in. "Well, hello. Ed, I fancy meeting you here. Can I join you?" She asked.

"You sure can" replied Ed. They sat there talking about the weather for a while. Cindy asked Ed if he caught any fish.

"I did, I caught two pompanos." Said Ed.

"Wow, they are good eating," she replied.

Ed thought for a moment. "Hey, maybe you'd like to come to my house some evening and have fish and chips sometime while you are down here."

"I would like to, but my girlfriend is in town with me, and we don't have much time here. We are here for six days."

"How long are you here for?" she asked him.

"Not sure yet. I came down to get away from the hassle with my Real Estate Office back home. I have been too busy for the past few years to have any time to do the things I want to." said Ed.

"Well, you will find this area here in Desitin a great place to enjoy and relax," Cindy said.

The waiter came over with a to-go sack and gave it to Cindy, who had pre-ordered it. Cindy got up and left after saying goodbye, saying, "Be seeing you around."

"I hope so," said Ed. Smiling at her.

Ed got up and got another cup of coffee and a donut. I love this place; It has a lot of things I like, he thought. He sat there for another 30 minutes just relaxing.

I think I need to go to the store and get some wine just in case I have some company. He got up, went to his car, and headed to Walmart. He bought some wine, potato chips, and cheese to go with the fish and some ice cream. He paid for his groceries and headed home and he put the food away.

The morning was still early. He had brought his golf clubs along. I think I'll play a round of golf this morning His clubs were still in his car. He drove over to the city golf course. When he got there, he took his clubs out of his car and went into the clubhouse, where he paid for a round of 18 holes. He went out, picked up his golf cart, tied his clubs on it then drove to the first tee.

There was a line. So, he fell into it behind a pretty lady walking with a pull cart. He watched her for a while and the ranger told her to ride with him.

She looked at him and the cart and said, "Sure, I will ride with you; I'm not very good, though."

"I'm not either." He spoke.

He tied her clubs onto his cart.

Ed was thinking, another pretty girl in two days. I love this place.

"You go first," Ed said. She teed up the ball, lined it up, and hit it 200 yards.

"Wow," said Ed, "That's a long way down the fairway. You must play a lot." Ed smiled at her and thought she was really pretty.

"My name is June. what's yours." She asked.

"I'm Ed, glad to meet you." They played and talked as they played golf.

"Do you play golf out here very often?" Asked Ed.

"Whenever I can," June answered. "Do you play here often?"

"No this is my first time playing here. It is a nice course." Said Ed.

Ed bogied the next 2 holes and pared the following 2. June was shooting par until she lost a ball in a pond. "Rats," she said.   They finished the 18th hole and were heading back to the cart house.

Ed asked. "You want to get a burger in the grill here."

"Sure, that sounds good and maybe a beer," June answered.

They drove the cart to their cars, put their clubs in it, put the cart away, and went to the grill. They ordered their burgers and a beer.

They sat down, and Ed asked her, "Are you from around here."

"Yes, I own a home here, and I've lived here for over 10 years," she said. "Do you live here?" she asked.

"No, I'm here for 2 weeks of rest and some fishing." Said Ed.

"Well, you should enjoy it here. There is a lot to do." Said June.

"I hope so," said Ed.

They finished their burgers and got up. "I've got to run. Maybe we will see each other on the course again," she said. They waved their goodbyes as they went to their cars.

Ed went back to the beach house, grabbed a beer, went to the deck, sat down, and watched some dolphins swimming in the waves. It was only 2:30.

He got up, grabbed his fishing pole and chair, and went to the beach. He sat down, picked up a shrimp from his bucket, and put it on his hook. He waded out a little and threw it a long way out. He stuck the pole in his holder and sat down.

It wasn't long before his pole bent way over and started pulling it out of the holder. He ran over and grabbed the pole and jerked on it to set the hook.

Ed started reeling hard, but the fish was pulling out of line. He reeled harder. Finally, after about 30 minutes, the fish started coming in but was still fighting.

He walked along the beach to tire the fish out. A crowd started gathering around to watch.

Ed did not notice as he was busy with the fish. Cindy had come by jogging and stopped to watch Ed. Ed finally got the fish close to shore and dragged it onto the shore. He has picked it up by the gills. It was a large redfish. He held it up, everyone was clapping.

Cindy came over to Ed and said "Nice catch, Ed. Can I take a picture of you holding the fish?"

Ed turned around and saw it was Cindy. "Ok," said Ed. He smiled at her.

She came over with her camera and aimed it at Ed, who held the fish up. Cindy took the picture. The crowd all started to leave, and Ed took the fish and released it back into the water. They all watched the large fish splash and take off.

"That looked like a lot of fun, Ed," said Cindy.

"Whew. It sure was," Ed replied as he sat down to rest.

"You want me to get another chair for you," said Ed.

"No, I need to get back. My friend is waiting to go shopping," Cindy said.

"Are you sure you and maybe your friend can't come over one evening for fresh fish and chips?" said Ed.

Cindy looked at Ed momentarily and said, "OK, when and what time?"

"Say around 7 o'clock. Tomorrow evening," Replied Ed.

"We'll be there. Do you want us to bring anything?" said Cindy.

"Nope." Said Ed.

"See you there," said Cindy.

They waved goodbye, and Ed sat down, watching her go away. Nice, he thought, smiling. She turned and smiled at Ed as she continued down the beach.

He reached out, baited his pole again, and threw it back into the surf. He sat back down in his chair, waiting for a bite. I Love this place. It has beautiful things, he thought.

Ed caught a couple more fish, picked up everything, and went inside. He cleaned the fish and then put them in the fridge. Ed cleaned the house up while thinking about the evening that Cindy and her friend were coming over. He put some oldies music on the radio. He made a sandwich, grabbed a beer, went to the deck, and sat until around 5:00 PM. He went back inside and cleaned the place up. He sat down, turned on the TV, and watched the local news for a while.

It started getting late and he got up and went to the fridge and got a small steak. He took it out to the grill. He sat there for a while. His steak was done. He sat down to eat it and enjoy the view. After a while, he picked things up, went inside with his beer, and enjoyed the rest of the evening. He cleaned things up and crashed for the night.

The following day, after cleaning up, Ed drove down to the Big Red Cafe and had bacon and eggs with his coffee. He sat there while watching all the people coming in. It looked like everyone was on vacation to enjoy the beaches.

He drove back to Bill's beach house. He poured another cup of coffee and went to the deck to drink his coffee. He sat there watching everyone going by, jogging, walking, and picking up shells.

He notices someone jogging. It was Cindy with her friend. She glanced up at him, smiled, and waved.

Ed waved back. They kept on Jogging. Ed smiled. After several minutes, Ed returned inside. I think I'll go out and drive around for a while to explore the area. He did and noticed the sign to the AFB.

He turned towards the base. He drove right on as he had his USAF ID card. He drove by the flight line and the BX. He saw the officers club. I'll have to go there soon.

He left the base and drove around the town, noticing places to eat and places with bands. He went by all the condos and the three golf courses. He saw a place called Andy's Seagull Lounge.

He pulled in and went in. Wow, he thought, this is an excellent place. It has a pool table, food and a band in the evening. He sat down at a table. The lady bartender came over. "What would you like to drink sir."

"I'll have a Bush beer on tap," Ed told her.

She brought the beer over quickly. He sat there for a while and looked at the pool table. He got up and went over to it. He put his two quarters in it and racked up the balls.

He selected a cue and went over to break the balls up. Just then someone came up behind him. He turns around. It was a cute, petite, blond, pretty girl.

"Could I shoot some pool with you?" as she was smiling at him.

"Sure, but I haven't shot any pool for a long time. "I'll break." Said Ed. He broke the balls up well.

A stripe went in. He lined up another stripe close to a pocket and knocked it in. He missed on his next shot.

She lined up a solid, knocked it in, and missed her next shot.

"I'm Julie. What's yours." She asked Ed.

"I'm" Ed. He replied.

"Glad to meet you," She answered.

"Same here," said Ed.

"You here on vacation? She asked

"Yep," as he lines up his next shot. He missed.

Ed took several sips of his beer as they were playing. There were cup holders on the side of the pool table.

She made her next shot. And she missed the next one. They played on until Ed scratched on the eight ball.

"Good game," said Ed.

"Nice meeting you," said Ed. "But I need to go.

"Maybe we will meet again said Julie.

"We might," said Ed, smiling. He left and drove back to the beach house.

He went into the beach house and looked around to see what he had to do for his dinner with Cindy and her friend. Looks like I don't need to do too much. He went out to the deck and sat until he was hungry. He went inside, made a ham sandwich, sat down, and watched the news and a couple of game shows until he got tired and went to bed. I love this place. You never know what you will do or who you will run into next.

The following day, he tidied up the place to prepare for Cindy and her friend coming over that evening. He looked around and thought the place looked good.

He went to his favorite place and had his coffee and breakfast at the Big Red Cafe. After breakfast, I will go to the fish market to pick up some fresh shrimp for tonight. I can make some shrimp cocktails for the ladies tonight.

He drove down to the fish market at the marina and bought some fresh shrimp that had already had their shells removed and were deveined. He picked up the bag and walked around the marina, which is a neat place. He hung out there for a while, as the shrimp were in an iced bag.

He saw a booth selling coffee and drinks. He went over, ordered a glass of sweet tea, and sat on a bench. He watched all the fishermen walking by with fish they had caught hanging by the charter boats. He sat there and thought I Love this Place.. I like to fish and will have to come back here.

He got up and drove back to the beach house. He went in and put the shrimp into the fridge. He made himself a cup of soup and poured a glass of iced tea. He went to the deck and ate his lunch. After lunch, he rearranged the table, chairs, and umbrella so they could set out on the deck this evening.

He went inside, put a tablecloth on the table, and arranged the chairs in case of rain or high winds. He set some dishes out and glasses. Looks good, he thought. He checked his wine and drinks. I think I'll walk the beach for a mile or so and get a little exercise. He headed out to the beach.

He headed west on the beach walking at a semi-fast beat. And every once in a while, they would pick up a nice shell. He watched the boats moving around, and he got back around 4:30.

He made a salad and set the fish out. He then fixed the shrimp cocktail and sat down until the news ended.

Ed returned to setting the table and preparing the fish for tonight. As he worked, a sense of contentment washed over him. All he had to do was cook the fish when Cindy and her friend arrived. He looked around at the place, feeling a deep satisfaction. It all looks good, thought Ed, and he couldn't wait for the evening to unfold.

It was only six o'clock, so Ed grabbed a beer from the fridge went out to the deck, and waited for them to arrive. I hope all goes well this evening. He sipped his beer and listened to waves. What a great place he thought.

He heard a car pull up under the house. He went to the door to greet them.

"Good evening, Cindy, come on in." said Ed'

"You are all dressed up and are looking great." Said Ed.

"Thanks. So do you." She replied. Ed had cleaned up and dressed neatly.

"This is my friend Mindy." Said Cindy.

"Glad to meet you, Mindy. What can I fix for you two? We have wine, beer, and bourbon." Said Ed.

"Wine will be fine," said Cindy.

Ed went over and poured two glasses of wine for them. "Let's go out on the deck and sit for a while.

He made himself a bourbon and coke. They went to the deck and sat in two chairs next to each other.

Ed raised his glass to Cindy and Mindy. "Cheers," he said. Cindy said, "Cheers, too," as she raised her glass.

Ed looked at Cindy and said, "You cannot get any better than this."

"You are right," said Cindy as she looked at Ed and thought nice smile, blue eyes, and nice hair.

"Where do you live in Tennessee? What do you do there? Asked Ed of Cindy.

"Well, I live in a small town in the Smokies called Lazy Daisy. I own a small book store called Read a Book Shop. How about you?"

"I live in the southern Indiana town of Ross Port, where I own my own real estate office, Martins Real Estate. I was just getting burned out with it. I'm on the phone all the time. I always had to work weekends showing houses. I decided to take some time off. Said Ed.

"Do you have a significant other? She asked.

"Nope, I dated some for a while; it didn't work out. I was married when I was young and she wanted a divorce. and I said yes. We were too young. After graduating from college, I joined the Air National Guard, where I retired as a colonel after twenty years, I was a pilot in the Guard. I flew the F4 most of the time." He answered.

"how about you?" asked Ed

Cindy said, "Well, I was married for 10 years, had no children, and he decided he wanted a divorce. Soon after the divorce, he married his secretary. I opened my bookstore twelve years ago, and it has done well.

My father bought the building several years ago, and my bookstore is in a portion of it. I live in the apartment upstairs. It is nice. On the other side, from the side next to my bookstore, I rent it out to an antique store. My father left the building for me, and I managed the rental myself.

I had a boyfriend for a couple of years. We broke up a couple of months ago.

He began to get possessive and I could not go anywhere without him checking up on me. He still bothers me sometimes and always wants to get back together. He's gone as far as I'm concerned."

They talked briefly, and Ed said, "Let's go have some fish and chips." They got up and went inside. Ed served up the shrimp cocktails first.

They were enjoying each other's company and smiling at each other.

"I hope you like the fish and chips." Said Ed.

Ed got up, fixed the fish and chips, and put them on their plates. "Enjoy, "said Ed.

"How about you, Mindy?" asked Ed.

"Well, I live in the same town as Cindy and work in her bookstore. I was married and now I've been single for a few years. I'm happy the way I am." Said Mindy

"If you are happy then you should stay that way. I'm sure someone will come along someday you will like." Said Ed.

"Cindy, would you like to come over tomorrow and go swimming with me? The water is great and warm, and we could sit on the beach for a while until it gets too hot," Ed asked.

"That sounds like a really good idea," said Cindy. "How about it, Mindy, you think I can get away for the day?

"Sure, I need to get some sun and beach time anyway. Have fun." Said Mindy.

"Say around 10:00 a.m. We could swim for a while then go grab some lunch around 10:30." Said Ed.

"Ok, that sounds like a plan." Said Cindy.

They finished eating. and Ed got up and started cleaning up.

"Here let me help you," said Cindy.

Cindy picked up her wine glass and bumped into Ed. "Whoops," she said and spilled all over Ed's shirt.

Ed looked down at his shirt and smiled. "No problem, I'll go put on another shirt, and then I'll finish this. He went into the bedroom and left the door ajar. Cindy continued cleaning up with Mindy's help.

Cindy noticed the door was open to Ed's bedroom, saw Ed taking off his shirt, and smiled. and thought nice body then looked away quickly.

Ed came out and found that they had finished the cleanup. Ed looked at Cindy and said, "I like having you around and doing things with you Cindy."

"I like being with you also." Said Cindy.

Mindy looked at them and smiled.

"We have only known each other for a couple of days, but they have been good. I've had trouble meeting someone that I can relate to," said Ed.

They stood close, smiling at each other, and Ed moved closer. "I better be going," Cindy said, moving towards the door.

"Come on, Mindy, It's getting late. Said Cindy smiling at Ed.

"It is getting late," said Ed. "See you tomorrow"

"I'll be here," she said and left.

Ed watched her go down the steps, and then he went inside, smiling. He went over and finished his glass of wine. Great Evening, he was thinking as he went into the bedroom for the night.

Ed got up, went out to the deck the following day, and stretched out his arms. Great day, he thought. He went inside and fixed some bacon and eggs. Poured himself a cup of coffee, went to the deck, and enjoyed his breakfast.

His phone rang, it was Bill from his office. "Hello, Bill," answered the phone.

"Hello, Ed, "Jim, his wife, my wife, and I are thinking about coming down next weekend for a short stay and some sun."

"That would be great," said Ed.

"How are you doing down there? Have you met anyone interesting yet?" Said Bill.

"Maybe," said Ed. "Let me know when to pick you up at the airport."

"Will do that," said Bill. "You didn't answer my question, Ed."

Ed laughed a little and hung up his phone.

He sat there thinking about the area and Bill's beach house. This is a great place, he was thinking. I think I will contact a realtor, as Indiana cooperates with Alabama, and look at a house and possibly buy one for myself. He finished his coffee and eggs and went back inside.

Yes, sir, that's what I am going to do. I'll talk to Bill about selling one of my rentals up north and start looking at houses on the beach next week.

Ed went to his car and drove over to Walmart to pick up some steaks for his company, which was coming this weekend. He also picked up some more wine and checked out.

Back home, he put the steaks in the fridge. Then, he straightened the place up, put on his swimsuit, and headed for the beach. He put the towels on two chairs he had on the beach. He walked into the water up to his shoulders. It felt good, and he floated around for a while when he heard someone yell.

"Hey there, you want some company out there." It was Cindy coming out onto the beach.

"You bet. Come on out. The water feels good." Said Ed. She came running out into the wave, looking fantastic in her swimsuit, thought Ed.

"This is nice." Said Cindy. "You been out here long?"

"Not long at all, just looking forward to you coming out." Said Ed.

"I was looking forward to this and seeing you again." She spoke.

Ed splashed water on her. "Hey, watch out there," she said, splashing back at him. They splashed around for a while, then went up to the chairs and sat there laughing and joking.

"I'll go in and get us some iced tea," said Ed. He got up and went in. He came out later with some sweet iced tea. He handed one to her and sat down on the deck chair.

"I've been thinking about buying my place and maybe settling here. "What do you think? Ed asked Cindy.

"I think that would be great," she said.

"Would you come down and visit me?" he asked her.

"I sure would. Would you get tired of me coming down all the time?" She answered back.

"Never," said Ed.

They sat there watching the people walk by and the shell seekers. Some were joggers and some were slow walkers—people of all sorts.

"Let's go into the house, then go out and get some lunch," said Ed.

"Sounds good," said Cindy

"Let's go down to the Back Porch restaurant I saw down the road." Said Ed.

"That sounds good." Said Cindy, "I'm kind of hungry after that workout in the water."

They got dressed and headed out the door, and Cindy said, "I'll follow you because I want to spend some time with my friend the rest of the day after lunch." Said Cindy.

They arrived at the restaurant and sat in a booth. The waiter brought over the menus and asked what they wanted to drink. "Coffee for me." Said Ed.

"Me too," said Cindy.

The waiter brought the coffee over and asked what she wanted to eat. "I'll have the Shrimp plate." Said Ed.

"I'll have the same," said Cindy.

While enjoying their lunch, Ed said, "I'm going to drive around and look at some houses for sale on the beach tomorrow."

'If you find one, I would like to look at it with you tomorrow." Said Cindy.

"That would be good" replied Ed. "I'll have to decide whether to move down here or use it as my getaway house." Said Ed.

"It would be great if you just moved down here," said Cindy.

After lunch, they said goodbye and left. Ed got back to the house and picked up the local real estate book he had picked up at the grocery store. He grabbed a drink and went to the deck to read the book. He marked a couple and headed out.

He drove west on the beach road and saw a large ranch home for sale that might work. He wrote the agent's name and house number down and drove on, finding two more by the same agent. He searched the agent's company address and returned to the beach house.

He entered the beach house, sat at the table, and pulled out his iPad. He looked up the first house online and then at the second. The second one was nice, and both were in his price range. He dialed the agent's phone.

"Hello," this is Anne.

"Anne, this is Ed Martin. I'm from Indiana. I'm a Broker there, and Alabama cooperates with us. "I am interested in your house on the beach called the Martini House. Is there any chance I can look at it tomorrow at 10 AM?"

"You sure can, and we will cooperate with you," said Anne. You will love that beach house. I will meet you there tomorrow."

"Great," said Ed, and he hung up. It was getting late, so he went to the fridge, grabbed a beer, and made a sandwich. He then went to the deck to watch the sunset. This is great. He finished his sandwich and went to bed.

The following day, he cleaned up, dressed in his smart real estate look, and ate a small breakfast of toast and peanut butter. He then took his coffee out to the deck and watched the waves.

I am thinking. I will sell off one of my apartment complexes back home to buy a beach house I have 4 of them. Save the rest of them for my income. I've owned them for over 30 years and they are all paid off.

He had called Cindy. It was 9:30 am and Cindy should be here soon. He went down to his car as Cindy drove up.

"Good morning," she said. And she got into his car.

"Good morning to you. too." He spoke. "You will like this house."

They drove to the house and the realtor was already there. "I have it all unlocked for you. Let's go on in." Anne said.

"This is a beautiful place," said Cindy.

They went up the stairs and inside. "Wow," said Ed.

They spent an hour looking it over. It had 3 bedrooms, 2 ½ baths and a nice kitchen. It needs some updating." How much will they take for this house? Asked Ed.

The book says $1.2 mil."

"you could just make an offer," Anne said."

"Ok," said Ed. "I will go back to the beach house where I am staying, think it over, and call you this evening."

"That will be great, I will be waiting for your call," said Anne

Ed and Cindy went back to the beach house. Ed picked up his phone and called Bill his co-broker.

"Hello" answered Bill.

"Hey Bill, I want to sell my apartments on 2nd street. Could you put them on the market for me? I'm asking for

$1.8 million for them. I'm going to buy me a beach house."
Said Ed.

"I will do that right away. It will sell fast as it is in a good area and always full," said Bill.

"Great I'll see you guys this weekend; we will have some fun," said Ed.

Ed hung up and sat down close to Cindy. He put his arm around her. They both smiled at each other.

"I think this is a good plan for me. I have done well enough in my real-estate business to live comfortably." Said Ed.

"Let's make a sandwich and sit on the deck for a while," said Ed.

"Ok" answered Cindy.

"After I get it, you will have to help me make some changes to the beach house," said Ed.

"I will, but I will be down here for only a few days, so don't forget," Cindy said.

"I know, "said Ed, "we will have to make the best of it, won't we?"

"You bet." Said Cindy smiling at him.

"I'll probably have to buy a boat to go fishing in.," said Ed.

"You will," Said Cindy "and you can teach me how to drive it."

"I could do that." Said Ed.

They sat on the deck for a while, and Ed said, "There is a small lounge down the road called The Red Door Saloon that has music after 4 this evening. Let's go there and have something to eat and drinks to relax and enjoy the music."

"I want to go, but I will drive myself ready, and I will meet you back here at 4," said Cindy.

Cindy got up and left saying "See you soon"

"Ed said "Ciao"

Ed sat there for a while and then got up. He cleaned up and combed his hair, humming a happy sound. He sat down and looked at the brochure, picked up the phone, and called Anne.

She picked up the phone "Hello"

"Anne, I want to make an offer on the beach house of $1.1 million." Said Ed.

"Ok, I will write it up right away." She spoke. "You must come over and put down the Ernest money."

"Ok, let me know." Said Ed and hung up.

He heard Cindy arrive. He got up and went down to meet her. They entered Ed's car and drove to the lounge, went in, and found a booth to sit in.

The waiter came over and asked what they wanted to drink. Ed looked at Cindy and asked, "How about martinis?" Cindy said "Great"

The waiter left and returned fast with their drinks. "Cheers". said, Ed.

"Cheers," said Cindy smiling.

"Ed looked at Cindy and said, "If you don't mind me saying, but I am getting to like you."

"I don't mind because I feel the same towards you." Said Cindy as she reached over and touched his hand.

Ed smiled at her.

The waiter came over and asked what they would like to order.

"I would like popcorn, shrimp, and fries," said Ed.

"I will have the same," said Cindy,

"Refills on our drinks," said Ed.

The band was about to start. The waiter brought out their dinner. They ate awhile talking about how much fun they had been having together. They almost finished their dinner, and the band played an Elvis song called Loving You.

Ed reached over and picked up Cindy's hand "Let's Dance."

They got up and Ed put his arms around her and pulled her close. They looked at each other for a few seconds and Ed moved closer to her. He started to kiss her, but she turned her head again.

"Ed, I would like to stay friends. I do like you, Ed." She kissed him on the cheek.

The music ended and they returned to their table holding hands.

"I enjoyed that song and dancing with you," said Ed. "I do want to stay friends with you too."

"I enjoyed it too." Said Cindy.

"Oh, I forgot to mention I made an offer on that beach house," said Ed

"Great now I can come down and visit often." Said Cindy.

"I would like that." Said Ed.

They continued dancing when songs came on that they liked for another hour or so. They finished their dinner. "That was a good time," said Cindy.

"It was," said Ed.

They left the lounge and headed back to the beach house. When they arrived, they exited the car and Ed approached Cindy.

Before Cindy got into her car Ed pulled her close to him and started to kiss her. She turned her head slightly for a peck on the cheek. She pulled loose and smiled.

They smiled at each other. Cindy rubbed Ed's arm and said, "Goodbye. Call me tomorrow after your friends arrive."

"I will," said Ed,

Cindy left waving and smiling at Ed. He went up the stairs and got ready for bed. He began thinking about Cindy and the events this weekend with his friends.

I know we are going fishing on Saturday morning. We could go to the lounge after we have our fish fry. He liked dancing with Cindy. He fell asleep dreaming.

The next morning, he got dressed had some eggs for breakfast, and went to the deck with his coffee. He sat out there looking at the time. His friends will arrive at 11:10. He watched the waves and thought about Cindy, hoping things would work out without hitches.

It was 10:15 when Ed headed over to the local airport. The plane had just landed when he entered the lobby. He watched them get off and met them at the luggage area.

They all did their greeting and hugs. Ed grabbed a couple of bags and said climb in." They loaded all the bags into his car and headed for the beach.

"OK, Ed. Tell us about this, Cindy. Do you like her? Will we meet her?" Jim asked.

"I do, and yes, you will meet her soon," said Ed. "I want to drive you by the beach house I want to purchase" Ed continued.

They drove over to the beach road and went a short way. He pulled into the driveway of the house. They all got out and went to the house's deck.

"Wow, this is great said Jim. They all walked down to the beach.

"I think I will enjoy fishing here and enjoying the area," said Ed.

They all went back to the car and Bill's beach house. After loading all the bags into the house. Ed fixed some sandwiches for lunch, and they all went to the deck to have a beer and sweet tea with their sandwiches. They all pulled up chairs and watched the waves coming in.

"I have us set up to go fishing on a private charter tomorrow. The boat can handle 6. How many want to go," said Ed.

The men said, "We do," and the ladies said, "We do too."

"How about your Cindy, think she would like to go with us." Said Bill.

"I'll call her," said Ed.

He dialed Cindy and she answered right away.

"Hello," said Cindy.

"Cindy, this is Ed. "Do you want to go fishing tomorrow on a charter with us?" said Ed.

"I would love to. Tell me where and what time." Said Cindy.

"Also, you want to go to the lounge tonight? Are we all going?" said Ed.

"sure," she answered.

OK. Come over at 6:30, and I will ride with you," Ed replied. We'll grab a bite to eat there."

They all sat there talking about how nice the area was.

"It is perfect down here for me." There is an Airforce base here, and I can use the BX there, as well as the

Commissary plus the club and their golf course," said Ed. "I Love this place."

"You'll have it made here. But how are doing with Cindy?" Said Jim.

Ed smiled "I love this place. I will have it made down here. I can't find anything wrong with it so far."

"We all are going to a little lounge down the road to get something to eat this evening and do a little dancing." Said Ed.

"That sounds great," said Bill.

They went inside and everyone went to their rooms to clean up for the evening.

Cindy arrived at 6 and knocked on the door. Ed went to the door and let her in. She went to the center of the room. Everyone came out of their rooms, ready to go, and went over and greeted Cindy.

"So glad to meet you," said Bill.

"We have heard many good things about you," said Jim.

The ladies hugged Cindy and said "So glad to meet you"

"I'm Betty," said Jim's wife.

"I Sue," said Bill's wife.

"You know Ed has had a hard time meeting anyone he likes for a long time' You must be special," said Mary, Bill's wife.

Cindy smiled and said, "So glad to meet all of you."

"Well let's all go out and have a good time together," Ed said as he was grinning. He put his arm around Cindy as they went out the door.

"You guys follow Cindy and me," said Ed.

They all jumped into their cars and headed out Ed was driving Cindy's car. They got to the lounge and went in.

Ed told the waiter that he needed a table for 6 where they could watch the band. The waiter nodded and gave them an excellent round table next to the dance floor.

The waiter came over "What can we get everyone for drinks." He passed out the menus.

The men all ordered a Busch beer. The ladies all looked at each other and decided they all wanted Martinis. The waiter left.

"I like this place," said Jim. "You been coming here often?

"Cindy and I have once," said Ed. Ed and Cindy looked at each other and smiled.

The waiter brought the drinks and passed them around. And asked if they were ready to order.

"Come back in a few minutes," said Ed.   The waiter left.

"So, Cindy, how did you meet Ed?" asked Bill.

"Well, I was jogging down the beach and saw this good-looking man fishing. I stopped and asked if he was catching anything. We talked a little bit and I continued down the beach." Said Cindy.

The waiter came over and took their orders. They all order the shrimp basket. He took their menus and left.

Sindy continued smiling at Ed. "We ran into each other at the donut shop later and began talking and that was it. We are now good friends."

"That's a good story," said Bill. "Things like that do not happen often."

The food arrived as they were talking about Ed and Cindy. They ate their dinner and talked about Ed and Cindy and the area.

They all finished their dinners. "That was some very good shrimp." Said Bill. The music started. The waiter came and picked up the plates and asked if they wanted refills on drinks.

"Yes," said Ed, his voice filled with a hint of excitement. Ed reached over and picked up Cindy's hand, a subtle yet significant gesture. They made their way to the dance floor, their steps mirroring the rhythm of their hearts. It was slow, fast. They danced a fox trot, their bodies moving in perfect harmony. The others, sensing the magic in the air, joined them on the dance floor.

Ed and Cindy held each other close on the next slow song. After the song was over, they sat down and sipped some of their drinks. The others sat down, smiling at them.

"Cindy looked at Ed and said, "You know I go home in 3 days."

"I know, "said Ed "We still have some time to spend together."

The others were looking at them, smiling.

They drank longer and danced some more until it was late.

Ed said, "It's late. We should go back to the beach house. They headed back and parked under the house. Ed went over to Cindy and hugged her.

"We will talk about things when we are alone. You will have to help me decorate my beach house. We are going fishing tomorrow; be here by 8.00."

Cindy nodded and left.

Ed went upstairs, and the others looked at him smiling.

Bill said, "I think you are getting serious about Cindy. Ed.

"I am, but we are just friends for now," said Ed. "it's late, and I'm going to bed."

They all go to their rooms, saying good night to everybody.

The following day, they all got up early. They ate a light breakfast and dressed to go fishing. Cindy arrived at 8:00 and met them downstairs. They drove in two cars to the marina.

The captain of the Black Eye boat was waiting for them. He welcomed them all aboard. He addressed them with safety instructions. and how to use the fishing gear. He introduced them to the deckhand. Ray. Ray gave them each a pole and showed them how to bait the hooks.

They all settled in as the boat left the marina. They looked at each other as the captain said, "Relax, as it will take us an hour to get out to the fish. The waves are calm today. You will have a good time. "The waves are less than 2 feet today, so it will be fairly smooth.

They arrived at the fishing spot, and the captain blew the horn. Drop your lines. They are at 30 feet. Count to three and lock your reel when you feel a slight yank pull up.

They dropped their lines.

Cindy yelled, " I got one as she was reeling hard." The deckhand went over and helped her get it aboard. It was a keeper a red snapper. He took it off the hook and put it in the cooler.

"Wow, that was a lot of fun and hard work. I need to sit down for a minute." Said Cindy. "That was exhausting."

Jim yelled I got one and brought it in. Ray took it off the hook and threw it in the cooler.

Soon, everyone was catching them. Ray was throwing some back because they were too small. They each got their limit in red snapper.

Ray said, "Pull your lines in. We are moving." They left the spot and drove for another 15 minutes.

"Ok," Ray said as he put some large bait on their hooks. "We are going after larger fish.

"Great," said Ed.

"Drop your lines," announced the Capt., "they are at 40 feet."

Everyone dropped their lines. It wasn't long before Jim yelled, "I got something on that is pulling hard."

Ray told him, "Just play him a little bit till he gets tired and reel him real slow."

Jim did what Ray had told him to do, and finally, he got to the edge of the boat. Ray brought over a gaff and brought the big fish aboard—a large Grouper.

"Wow," they all said.

"Is it a keeper?" asked Ed.

"Yes," said Ray, they are in season now.

They fished for another half hour, and the Capt. announced, "Reel them in. We are going back to the marina."

They all sat down, discussing what a great time it was. They arrived at the Marina and disembarked. Ray gathered their fish and began cleaning them while Ed and his friends watched. After he was done, he put the fish in a cooler and gave it to Ed.

Ed gave Ray a good tip.

"Let's take these fish to the Harbor Tavern that I like to go to and give the fish to the chef. He will cook them up for us this evening," said Ed.

They drove over to the Tavern, and Ed took the fish to the chef. He returned and said, "Let's go home and clean up and have some drinks on the deck, rest up awhile."

"Good idea," said Cindy. "I'm exhausted."

Ed looked at her and smiled. She smiled back.

When they returned to the beach house, they all disappeared to their rooms; Cindy went to Ed's room while he grabbed a beer and went to the deck.

Cindy came out 2 minutes later and said, "It's all yours now."

Ed got up, "Thank you," and disappeared.

It wasn't long before everyone was on the deck with their drinks. They all were laughing and enjoying the view of the gulf.

It was only 12:30. Ed told everyone they could go in, make sandwiches, and rest for the evening.

"We will leave about 6:30 for the Tavern," said Ed.

"I think I will go back to my condo, change clothes, and meet you at the Tavern. I know where it is, OK?" said Cindy.

"Sure," Said Ed. "get some rest."

Cindy left.

Everyone crashed into their rooms at the beach house for a while, tired from fishing in the hot sun. Around 4, they all started to get up and came into the living room. They sat around talking about how much fun the fishing trip was.

Bill looked at Ed and said, "We will close on your apartment house next week, and the money will go directly to your bank account."

Jim said, "The real estate business is doing well, and I think it will continue as it has for a long time."

"Great," said Ed. I want to close on my beach house in about ten days. The inspection will be done by this Wednesday. "I want to get started on the changes that I want and buy some new furniture. I hope Cindy will help with the choices," said Ed.

"I think you are going to like it down here. Are you going to keep your house up north?" Said Jim.

"I think I will for a while." Said Ed.

"I might want to go back in the summers."

"You can let Jim and I know what you want to do with your share of the business down the road." Said Bill.

"I will do that." Said Ed.

"Let's go over and have our fish and chips," said Ed.

They all left and headed over to the Tavern. Cindy was waiting. That's a nice thought, Ed. They went in, and the waiter seated them at a round table. He asked what they wanted to drink.

"Busch beer for us guys and wine for the ladies. Said Ed.

The waiter left.

"We go home tomorrow," said Bill," "I wish we could stay longer, but some of us have to work."

"I sure don't miss work, "said Ed.

"I don't have to leave until Friday," said Cindy.

Good you can help me pick out my new furniture for my Beach house," said ED.

Their fish came along with their drinks, and they began eating and talking about how much fun it had been down here on the beach.

They finished eating and had two more drinks.

"It's getting late," said Bill "We have to catch our plane in the morning."

They all got up and left. Ed approached Cindy as she was about to get in her car. He pulled her close and said, "I'll see you in the morning."

"You will for certain." Said Cindy.

They all left and went to the beach house, where they crashed for the night. Ed thought about shopping with Cindy the next day and went to sleep.

Ed woke up the following day and got dressed. The others came out with their bags. Ed took them all to the airport and said goodbye. Ed headed back to the beach house. He went in and noticed he had left his phone there. It had a message on it.

It was Cindy "Ed, I have to go back home this morning as my mother is sick and in the hospital. I will call you when I get home."

He sat down, not knowing what to do. I guess I will go pick out the furniture myself and hope all goes well with Cindy, He thought.

He made himself some bacon and eggs, got a cup of coffee, and went to the deck and sat down watching the waves missing Cindy already.

The phone rang it was Anne. "Hello," said ED.

"You bought yourself a beach house. Come in and sign this offer," she said.

"OK, I'll come down this morning.

After his breakfast, he went down to the Realtor's office and signed the offers. And kept one copy. He left her the Ernest money check.

He went to the furniture store and selected all the furniture for the house he wanted. He then went down to the real estate office and checked to see if the inspection had been ordered. He had forgotten about that when he was there. It had been ordered.

The inspection was not to be done until tomorrow at 10:00. Ed decided to go down to meet with him and watch. He went back to Bill's beach house. He also looked over the signed offer to make sure he had not missed anything. It all looked good.

He went to the deck and called Cindy. She answered right away. "Well, hello, ED"

"Hello Cindy, I was just calling to see how things are with your mom; I hope you're well. I am also calling to tell you that I have bought a beach house.

"Fantastic said Cindy, My Mom is getting better now and back home. We will watch her for a few days to see how she does."

"Good. I have purchased some furniture. If she gets well enough, maybe you can come down and help arrange it," said Ed.

"I will let you know. Talk to you soon." Said Cindy and hung up.

Ed sat there for a while, went inside, and fixed himself some lunch and went to the deck. He spent the afternoon on the deck looking at boats online. He thought that he might have to talk to someone who knows about boats.

It was late afternoon, and he went to the fridge. He pulled out a steak and put it on the grill. He sat down with a beer until the steak was done and went inside to enjoy it. He cleaned up and then crashed for the night.

The next morning, after breakfast, he headed down to his beach house to meet with the inspector. The inspector was there when Ed got there. He asked the inspector if he could follow him around. He said it would be okay, but not to talk. Ed followed him around as the inspector was writing things down.

When they finished, The inspector turned and said, "I am sending this report to Anne now. You can go there to pick it up."

"Ok said Ed. He left and went to the real-estate office, picked up the report, and a key to the beach house. He went back home where and sat down to read it. He noticed a couple of things that required attention. They were the HVAC was not working and Dishwasher was broken.

He called his realtor about those that needed to be fixed right away, as he was going to move in on Wednesday after closing.

His realtor said, "I've taken care of it".

He sat down and was watching the TV when Anne called him back

"The items on the inspection will be fixed tomorrow. Anne said.

Ed said "Good, I'm meeting with a Good Will person soon to have some of the old furniture removed.

"Thank you." Said Ed. "I need the number of a carpenter to make some changes in the house."

Anne paused and said "Call Bud on this number"

"Thanks," said Ed and hung up.

I'm really hungry, and he drove down to the diner, grabbed a bite to eat, went back to Bill's beach house, sat down, and rested for a while. He picked up his phone and called Bill.

Bud answered "Hello."

"Hello, my name Is Ed and I need a carpenter at my beach house. I need some changes on the inside. Are you available?" said Ed.

"I am in between jobs right now and have some time. I'm Bud." Said Bud "I can meet you at your house anytime."

"How about tomorrow at 9 am" Bud replied.

"Fine" see you there," said Ed. He gave Bud the address and hung up.

Ed grabbed a beer and went to the deck and watched the waves roll in. he went back in fixed some dinner and crashed for the night,

The next morning, he went down to his beach house to meet Bud. Bud arrived shortly after he did. Ed introduced himself and Ed replied, "I'm Bud."

"Come on in, Bud, and I will show you around," said Ed.

They went in, and Ed took him to the shower and told him to make it a walk-in shower and tear out the one. Then he went to the kitchen and asked, "Can you replace this countertop with granite?" said Ed.

"I can and do want a new sink and faucets?" said Bud.

"Yes," said Ed "Here is a sample of granite I want and sink and faucets."

"Great," said Joe. " I'll get you a quote tomorrow."

"Ok, here is my phone number text me with the quote and time to complete the job," said Ed.

Ed looked the place over and went back to Bill's Beach house.

He grabbed a beer, went to the deck, sat down, and began thinking about Cindy. I sure do miss her. He was sitting on the lounge and fell asleep.

It was 4:00 when he woke up still holding his beer. He looked around and yawned big and finished his beer. He got up and went inside. I think I'll go down to the little The Harbor Tavern and get myself a burger and fries.

He arrived at the bar, went inside, and sat down in a booth. The waiter came over and said, "I think I recognize you from the other night dancing with a pretty girl."

"Yep, that was me." Said Ed.

"I need a burger with ketchup, cheese, and onion on it and a sweet tea". Said Ed.

"You got it," said the waiter. He brought the sweet tea over right away.

Ed sat there looking at the dance floor picturing himself dancing with Cindy.

Just then his phone rang. "Hello," said Ed.

"Ed this is Cindy, "what are you doing now, I sure miss you,"

"I miss you too. I'm sitting at a bar having a burger and fries." said Ed, "How are things going there."

"Not good," said Cindy. I have some things to work out with Mom and my sister. We have to work out some care for her before I can come down again. I also have to work out what to do about my shop.

"You take care of things there first, and then we can figure out what we want to do, OK?" said Ed. We will stay in touch often.

"We will," she replied.

"Take care, Ed," she said and hung up.

His burger just arrived. He drank some of his tea, picked up his burger, and took a big bite, smiling about Cindy. He finished his burger, paid his tab, and headed back to the beach house.

It was getting late, so he decided to hit the sack. He relaxed, dreaming a little. I Love this Place.

The next morning, at 6 a.m., he woke up. He showered and dressed. Ed went to the kitchen, ate a light breakfast, and had a cup of coffee on the deck. He then went down and put his golf clubs in the back of his SUV.

It was a lovely day in Destin to play golf. He arrived at the golf course at 9:05, entered the clubhouse, and paid his fees. When he got to the number on the tee, there were three guys in line.

Ed asked them, "Can I join your group."

They all looked at Ed, and one said, "Be glad to have you."

"My name is Ed," said Ed.

"I'm Joe and this is Fred and Phil. Glad to meet you, Ed," said Joe. They all teed off, and Ed rode with Phil.

"What did you do in life?" said Phil.

Ed replied, "I retired from the Air Force as a Colonel after 20 years and own my own real estate office in Indiana."

"I'm a Capt. here at Destin Airforce base. Been here 15 years and plan on retiring here, Said Phil.

"I'm buying a beach house here and plan on retiring here also." Said Ed.

They all took turns driving on the first tee box.

They arrived at the 1st green, and they all put out. As they were playing, they discussed their military lives. They talked about the different planes they had or were flying and their positions in the military. They finished the golf round at 11:15

"We're going to the Officers Club. Want to join us? "Said Joe.

"Sure," said Ed.

"we'll meet you there," said Joe.

Ed nodded. He got in his car and drove not very far onto the base. To get on the base, Ed had to show the guards his military ID. He drove over to the Officers Club; the guys were already there. They entered the club and sat down at a table by the bar.

Joe said, "They are having a shrimp special today for $6 bucks."

The waiter came over and they all ordered a draft beer.

"How long are you staying here?" asked Fred.

"I just purchased a beach house. I'm closing on it soon. I plan on retiring down here."

"That's great said Joe.

The drinks arrived and the waiter took their order of the shrimp dinner. They all began eating and drinking their beer.

"How did you pick this area, Ed," said Phil.

"I was stationed here on a couple of exercises before I retired as a colonel from the USAF and the Air National Guard. I loved it down here." Replied Ed.

"That's great," said Joe. "Keep us in mind when you want to play golf. We have a men's league here on Thursdays. Think about it."

"I will," said Ed.

They finished eating and they said their goodbyes. Ed went back to the beach house as the phone rang. It was Bud.

"Hello," said Ed.

"I have your estimate for you," said Bud

"Ok, give it to me," said Ed.

"I can do everything, including the granite top, for $7,200." Said Bud.

"OK, Email the written estimate. You can start tomorrow afternoon at 1:00. I will be there to let you in," said Ed.

"good," said Bud.

Ed hung up, grabbed a beer from the fridge, and went to the deck. He began thinking about how Cindy was doing. He sat here for a while and grew tired. He went in and crashed on the couch. He was napping for a time when his phone rang.

"Good afternoon, Ed," said Cindy.

"Oh, hello Cindy. It's good to hear your voice. How are things going for you?" Ed said.

"Things are getting better. Mom is back home and getting better. My sister said she would see to her needs and keep looking for a good nursing home for when I am gone down there to see you. I am still considering selling my shop and the building." Said Cindy.

"Wow, that sounds like a plan. Make sure that's what you want to do. If that would make you happy." Said Ed. "I close on my beach house Wednesday morning, and I am meeting the carpenter at 1 to start fixing the things I want done.

"I'm anxious to see the things you changed in the beach house and the new furniture." Said Cindy

The new furniture is to arrive Friday morning." Said Ed.

"You know, Ed, I do miss you and want to get down there to spend some time with you," Cindy said.

"I miss you a lot and want you to come down so we can spend some time together," said Ed.

"I want to come down before I consider selling my shop. Mindy gave me some options that sound good. She will manage the shop and the rental. Said Cindy.

"I'm anxious for you to come down and see what I'm doing with my beach house," said Ed.

"I'm going to hang up now Cindy. Goodbye," said Ed. "I'm looking forward to seeing you again."

"Oh, Ed." Goodbye and hung up.

Ed went to bed feeling happy. He wanted to be near her and hold her in his arms.

The next morning, he got up in a good mood, cleaned up, and ate some breakfast. He drank his coffee on the deck while waiting to go to the closing of his beach house.

He finished his coffee and headed to the closing company a little early to review the Hud statement. Anne was there waiting for him. They sat down, and Ed looked over the Statement, checking to ensure she had included his broker fee. It had. Everything else looked fine. He had already transferred the funds to the closing company account.

Ed and the seller signed the forms at the closing, and the deed was handed over to Ed. Everyone was happy, and Ed smiled he is the the proud owner of a beach house. He put the keys into his pocket and left, heading to his beach house.

When he got to his beach house, he walked through it to see if the seller had fixed the problem areas. They had. He picked up his phone and called the Salvation Army to come and pick up all the old furniture. He kept some things.

I think Cindy will like this place with me, I hope things work out with us, he was thinking. He walked out to the deck, sat down on a deck chair, and watched the waves crashing on the shore.

He heard a truck pull up under the house. It was Bud. He was early, hoping to get started on the job. He came in and they shook hands.

"Good to see you, Bud. You remember what I want done. You can have a go at it. Just do a good job for me," said Ed.

"I will do that," said Bud and he set his tools down and headed to start in the shower.

Ed waited for the Goodwill people to come. They arrived shortly, and Ed went over everything that was to be going. They began moving furniture out right away. Ed went out and sat on the deck for a while. They came out and said, "We're all done. Here is a receipt for all the furniture." They left.   Ed told Bud, "I'm leaving the door unlocked for the day; I will come back this evening and lock up."

"Ok," said Bud.

Ed left and went to the base to the Officers' club to grab a bite. When he entered, his golf friends were there. "Can I join you fellows?" said Ed.

"Have a seat," said Phil. "Did you get closed on your beach house?"

"I sure did and I have a carpenter there doing some remodeling for me." Said Ed.

"You will have to have us over when you are all done and have a cookout." Said Joe.

"I will do that," said Ed.

They all had a special for lunch: club sandwiches and chips. They were leaving when Joe said, "We are Going On a fishing trip next Tuesday. Can you join us?"

"I would love to. What time and where?" said Ed.

"Meer us at the marina at 8:00." Said

Joe.   They all said their goodbyes and went to their cars.

"See you then," said Ed.

Ed drove back to Bills Beach House and did some laundry. And had a beer on the deck. I must buy linens, towels, and miscellaneous stuff for my beach house. I need to call my home insurance company for my beach house. I need to have the utilities will be changed also.

He spends the rest of the afternoon on the phone, taking care of the insurance and utilities. In the morning, I need to go to Walmart and get the linens and stuff for the beach house and some groceries. He was thinking about what else he needed to do about the beach house.

He left and went over and locked up the beach house for the night, then went back to Bill's beach house. That evening, he had a sandwich and watched some news before going to bed. He was tired.

The following day, he went down and met Bud at his beach house and unlocked it. Then, he went to Big Red Cafe, where he had bacon and eggs for breakfast. Then he returned to his beach house and waited for the new furniture to arrive. He didn't have to wait long before it arrived.

The men placed the furniture in the correct rooms where Ed wanted them and left. Ed went in and checked on Bud and the shower. Bud had removed the old shower and started on the walls for the new shower.

"Good Job," said Ed.

"Thanks, no problems so far." Said Bud.

Ed left and headed for Walmart. He bought two carts full of Linens and stuff. While he was putting it all in his SUV, he remembered he needed to call about getting a lift (elevator) installed in the beach house. He got to the beach house and spent a long time lugging it all up the stairs and putting it away.

After he was done, he was exhausted. He grabbed a cold beer from his fridge and went to the deck. And he sat down with his phone. He called Anne, his realtor, and got the name of someone to install a lift in his beach house.

He dialed the number. "Custom Lifts of Destin, how can I help you?"   "Yes," Ed said, giving him the address of his beach house. "I need a lift installed at my beach house."

"We can do that; when can we meet? My name is Red."

"How about this afternoon," said Ed.

"Ok, we can be there at 2:00." Said Red.

"That will work," said Ed.

Ed thought I have enough time to run down and get a burger. He left and drove down to the Big Red Cafe, went in, and sat down.

The waiter came over and asked what he wanted to drink. Ed said, "How about an iced tea and a toasted burger with cheese, onion, and ketchup on it."

"I'll bring that right out to you." Said the waiter."

It wasn't long till the waiter brought out the tea, and his burger. Ed enjoyed the burger, sitting there, thinking about his future. He finished his burger, drove back to his beach house, and waited for Red, the lift installer.

Red was right on time and Ed let him in the door.

Red said, "Where would you like this lift installed?"

"Right over here, it looks like a good spot, but it's out of the way since I have a very large living area. I would like the door to open towards the living room and be about 2.5 x 3.5 feet if that is a normal size," said Ed.

Red looked at the area and took some measurements. "That's a normal size," said Red. Let me go downstairs and look around." Red left and went down with Ed.

Red looked it all over where the lift would go. "It would work here." He spoke. "Let's go upstairs and talk about what kind you want."

They went upstairs and sat on the new couch. Red brought out some brochures. "We have two kinds of cable on and a hydraulic one."

Which one would you recommend, and which one would require less maintenance and be fault-free?" Said Ed.

"I would recommend the cable one, as all the hardware would be up against your ceiling since you have 10-foot ceilings," said Red.

"How about an extended warranty," said Ed.

"It would come with a 5-year warranty, parts, and labor, not including hurricane damage." Said Red.

"What would the total cost be?" Said Ed.

Red pulled out an estimate sheet and wrote down a bunch of figures. Red looked at Ed and asked, "What kind of door does he want, a steel door or solid wood door, both with safety latches? I would recommend the solid wood door stained to match your decor."

"Ok, the wood door," said Ed.

Red finished with the estimate and handed it to Ed. Ed looked it over and read the $7,000.

Red said, "We can start tomorrow if that is all right. It will take us about 6 days to complete It."

"OK, go ahead and get started. Send me an invoice." Said Ed.

Ed went back to Bill's beach house and went in, but his phone rang. It was Cindy.

"Hello, Cindy." Said Ed.

"Ed, I'm almost down there to see you for the weekend if that will be all right." Said Cindy.

"Great, what time will you be here?" Said Ed.

"About 8:00." Said Cindy.

"I'll have something to eat for you when you get here." Said Ed.

"I'll be Glad to see you then," Cindy said.

Ed jumped up, went to the fridge, and pulled out a couple of pork chops. It was almost 6:00. He put the pork chops in a bag of salt and pepper and put them back into the fridge. (Brineing) He made a salad and put it in the fridge. Grabbed a beer and went to the deck smiling. He was looking forward to Cindy being here.

He sat there, got up at 7:30, and went into the kitchen to prepare the salad and pork chops.

Cindy arrived at 7:48 and went into the beach house and surprised Ed.

Ed turned and smiled, ran over, and picked her up, hugging her. "I'm so glad to see you," Ed said. He sat her down, smiling at her.

"You want something to drink," said Ed.

"Yes, how about a gin and tonic." Said Cindy.

"You sit down and rest for a minute." Said Ed.

Cindy sat down, watching Ed fix her drink. He fixed one for himself, brought the drinks over, and sat down on the couch beside her. He handed her the drink.

"Cheers said Ed as they touched their glasses together."

"How was your trip down," said Ed.

"Easy not much traffic." Said Cindy.

"Great," said Ed. He got up and said, "I'm fixing us some pork chops and a salad. It will be ready in about 10 minutes."

Cindy got up also and went to the kitchen. "How can I help?" she asked.

"You can put the salad in a couple of bowls and set them on the table." Said Ed.

She did, and Ed said the pork chops were done. He put them on a plate and sat them on the table.

"Enjoy," said Ed.

They sat down at the table with their drinks and began eating.

"These are good pork chops," said Cindy.

"Thanks," said Ed.

"Are things going well at home?" asked Ed.

"I think so. We are getting Mom settled now, and my sister and I are looking at a rest home for her." Said Cindy.

"That is a good idea," said Ed.

After they finished their dinner and cleaned up the dishes, they went to the couch with refilled drinks.

"Want to watch a movie? Said Ed.

"Sure," Cindy replied.

"Ok, how about a romance movie on the new AGFC channel." Said Ed.

Ed found one and started the movie. They sat close to each other, Ed's arm around Cindy's shoulder and Cindy's head on his shoulder. They had finished their drinks and were watching the movie, and Cindy fell asleep.

Ed watched the movie for a while, then turned the TV off. He moved slowly away and up from Cindy and placed her head on a pillow on the couch. He covered her up with a cover. He looked at her and smiled.

Ed turned out the light and went to bed.

Cindy awoke the following day and sat up. She stretched out her arms and yawned. She looked around and smiled. She went over and made a cup of coffee with the pod maker. She took her coffee, went to the deck, sat, and watched the waves.

It wasn't long before Ed came out with his coffee and sat down beside her in a chair.

Ed looked at Cindy and said, "You sleep well?"

"Yes, I did, Thanks." Said Cindy.

"After breakfast, let's go over to my beach house and see how they are doing with the remodeling." Said ED.

"Ok," said Cindy.

"You want to go down to the cafe for breakfast or here?" said Ed.

"Okay, let's go down to the cafe," Cindy said. But I want to clean up first."

Cindy got up and went to the guest bedroom to clean up. She took her suitcase with her.

Ed waited on the deck for her to emerge. After about 30 minutes, she emerged smiling.

"Let's go get breakfast," she said.

They went down, got in Ed's SUV, and drove to the diner. They sat in a booth. The waiter came right over and asked what they wanted to drink.

"Coffee for me," said Ed

"Same here," said Cindy.

The waiter left and came back with their coffee. "What can I get you two for breakfast?" he asked.

"I will have biscuits and gravy," said Ed.

"Same here, only a half order." Said Cindy.

"I'm sure glad you came down for the weekend. "Said Ed.

"Me too." Said Cindy.

The waiter brought over their breakfast. They sat there while Cindy talked about what was happening at home.

"I don't know how long before I take care of everything." Said Cindy.

"Don't worry about it. We have a lot of time. Do what you have to do," said Ed.

They finished their breakfast and headed over to his beach house. The workers were all there. They entered and talked to the two guys who were installing the lift.

"How's it going?" asked Ed.

"Just fine one of them," he said.

"We should finish up today."

"Great," said Ed.

They went into the master bath where Bud was working. Bud looked at them and said, "I will finish up here tomorrow and start working on the countertops tomorrow afternoon. I will have my plumber come over to plumb and install the sink."

"That will work for me as I would like to move in this weekend. Said Ed.

Cindy said, "I would like to be here but can't. I'm heading back home in the morning."

"I wish you could stay, but I understand. I'm glad you're here for the day," said Ed. "Maybe you could help me with the colors for the Kitchen, living room, bedrooms, and baths."

"I can do that," said Cindy, walking around, looking at all the rooms, and making some notes.

"Let's go over to Home Depot now and pick out the paint." Said Ed.

"Ok, boss she bumped him, smiling at him.

They went to the car, headed to the Home Depot, and went inside to the paint department. Cindy picked up a chart of satin paint colors.

"I like this for the kitchen, this for the living room, this for the bedrooms, and this for the bathrooms. "Said Cindy

Ed was writing all this down. He then took the paint chart over to the paint clerk and showed him the colors he wanted and how much of each. The clerk started working on it right away.

Ed had picked up a cart on the way in. "Let's get some paintbrushes and some plastic covers in case we have to use some of it. I plan on hiring a paint crew to do it real soon. Anne gave me the name of a painter. I will call tonight," said Ed.

The clerk had the paint all gathered up and stirred up, ready to go. Ed put it all into the cart and got it into his SUV. He headed to his beach house.

Ed and Cindy carried everything up the steps and stored it all in the middle of the living room out of the worker's way. They sat down on the couch and rested, watching the workers come and go. Then they went out to the deck and sat awhile.

Ed looked at Cindy. "There is an art show going on today down near the beach about 2 miles away. Do you want to go to it?" he asked her.

"That's a good idea. I like art shows, but you need a couple of nice pictures of your beach house." She answered.

They went to Ed's SUV and drove a few miles to the art show on the beach. The art show is set up by the area's local artists.

Ed got a parking spot close to the show. They got out, went to the entrance, and walked in. They strolled along, looking at all the artists' booths.

"Oh, look at cute little puppies," Cindy said.

There were several people there with small dogs.

"Maybe I'll get me a small puppy someday." Said, Ed

"I like dogs," said Cindy.

Cindy walked into a booth that had some nice beach oil paintings.

"Oh, Ed, come look at this one." It was a painting of the seashore with a couple walking down the beach against the sunset." Said Cindy.

Ed came over and looked at the painting.

"That's a really good picture. Kinda romantic, isn't it" he said." He held her while they both looked at it and smiled at each other. "Let's buy it, and it will look nice in my living room."

He paid the lady in the booth for the picture. It was a nice size, 24 x 36 on canvas, a no-frame picture. The lady put it in a large paper sack.

They continued down through all the booths when Cindy again said, "Ed, here are some pictures that would look good in the bathrooms." Ed came over and looked at the different pictures of shrimp boats out in the gulf.

Cindy said, "I like these two, don't you."

"Yes, I do, I'll buy both of them."

He paid the attendant who put them into a sack for them. Ed took them, and they continued and decided to grab something to eat. There was a food truck there that had small shrimp plates.

That sounded good. They ordered two plates and some iced tea and sat down at a table. They talked about the pictures and where to hang them.

After finishing their shrimp, they decided to Go back to Bill's beach house and walk on the beach.

At the beach house, Cindy picked up a hat to wear on the beach and changed her shoes. Ed did the same. They put on their sunglasses and headed to the beach.

"It's a great day here on the beach," said Ed.

"It sure is. I love coming down here and enjoying the beach, especially with you." Said Cindy.

Ed looked at her and smiled. Cindy had taken her shoes off and was walking where the waves were washing up on the beach.

"Oh, look, there is a big whole shell," she said.

She picked it up, looked at it, and handed it to Ed to carry. Ed smiled and took it. She found two more, and Ed carried them all.

They walked a little further, and Cindy looked at Ed and said, "If I get things worked out with my mom, I would like to come down and spend a week with you."

"I think we could work that out" as he put his arm around her shoulders and squeezed her slightly. Smiling.

They turned, their footsteps sinking into the warm sand, and made their way back to the beach house. The sun was beginning its descent, casting a golden hue over the ocean. Ed suggested, "Let's head to The Harbor Tavern. They have good burgers there. We can enjoy the live music that starts around 6 tonight."

"I'd love that," said Cindy.

They went to their separate rooms, cleaned up, and changed clothes. Ed came out and was waiting on Cindy. She came out and Ed looked at her.

Ed's eyes lit up as he saw Cindy. "You look stunning," he complimented her.

"You do too with that sport coat on." Said Cindy.

They drove to the tavern, went in, and sat at the same booth they had sat in once before. The waiter came over and asked, "What can I get you for drinks?"

"How about a couple of chocolate martinis" said Ed as he was looking at Cindy.

"That will be fine'" she said.

"Are you anxious to get in your new Beach house?" Said Cindy.

"I am. I hope I can get in next weekend or before then. When I do I plan on having the group come back from up north and have a housewarming party." Said Ed.

"Wow, I don't know if I can get away that soon." Said Cindy. "I will try."

"Good'" said Ed. Their drinks came.

They sat and talked about things that they could do together.

"We could go sailing or golfing. I used to play some golf and I still have my clubs." Said, Cindy.

"There are lots of things to do down here. That's what I like about this place.

"You know, I have not decided what to do with my shop yet." Cindy said, "I'm still really cautious."

"I can understand that and I plan on going slow so we can get to know each other better." Said Ed.

The burger and fries arrived. They looked at each other, smiled, and took some bites out of the burgers.

"I believe things will work out because I like you more than you can imagine," said Ed.

Cindy smiled at Ed and said," I'm glad, I feel the same way."

They finished eating. The music started.

Just then, a lady approached them. It was June from the golf course.

"Hello Ed, remember me from the golf course."

Kind of shocked, Ed looked up and said, "I do."

He looked at Cindy, who was wondering who this lady was,

"Cindy, this is June, who I met on the Golf course. The ranger paired me up with her a week ago when I went golfing alone." Said, Ed

"June This is Cindy, my very close friend." Said Ed.

"Glad to meet you," said June.

"Cindy said, "Nice meeting you, June."

Ed felt uncomfortable.

June said, "Nice seeing you again, Ed and meeting you, Cindy."Are you enjoying yourselves here? This is a nice place to eat and dance. Me and my friends come here whenever this band is playing, they are really good." She spoke.

Ed said, "We are enjoying ourselves here and have come here a couple of times. It is a very nice place."

"Have a good evening," she said. "I need to get back to my friends it's Girl's night out." She left.

Cindy looked at Ed and said Is this someone I should worry about."

"Nope, not at all." Said Ed sternly. "The only time I met her was at the golf course and the only time I ever saw her."

"No worries, you are the only one for me." Said Ed. And he smiled at Cindy. The band began playing.

Cindy smiled. Ed reached over, took her hand, and said, "Let's dance; I love this song. It's one of Elvis's love songs."

They got up, went to the dance floor, and Ed pulled her close. They danced like they had feelings for each other.

"I just love holding on to you." Said Ed.

"I love you holding on to me. You are an excellent dancer," said Cindy.

Cindy smiled at him.

They danced a few songs and then headed back to the beach house.

"You want a nightcap." Said Ed'

"Yes.' Said Cindy.

They sat on the couch and watched another romance movie, not talking a lot as the movie was good after the movie. They hugged each other good night and went to their rooms alone.

The following day Cindy had packed her suitcase and was drinking a cup of coffee when Ed came out.

"Good morning said Cindy. "You slept in a little."

"I did. I guess I was tired.," he said. "You want some breakfast before you leave. I hate to see you go."

"I want to ask if you can stay an extra day. I want to look at boats today. I would like for you to go with me." Ed said.

Cindy looked at Ed and considered it. "I'll call my sister and tell her I won't return until tomorrow."

She called her sister and it was all right.

Ed smiled. Let's get breakfast, go to the marina, and look at boats. "I have an idea of what kind I want.

"let's go to the marina and have breakfast there." Said Ed.

"Sounds like fun. I'll get an extra day with you" she said smiling at him. He smiled at her, too.

They headed towards the marina. "It looks like a great day to look at boats with you," Ed said. They saw a café across from the marina and pulled in. They went inside.

A waiter approached to seat them in a booth and gave them a menu. "What would you like to drink," he said.

"Coffee for us both'" Ed said as Cindy nodded.

The waiter returned with the coffee and asked what they wanted to eat.

"I want a Belgium waffle and a piece of bacon." Said Ed.

"Same here, "said Cindy.

They talked about boats and fishing till breakfast came. They enjoyed their breakfast together and left for the marina. Ed parked right up next to a few places with boats for sale.

They got out and walked around. They stopped at one that had had a sign out about the sale inside. They went in and looked around a little until a salesman came and asked if he could help them.

Ed looked at the salesman and said, "We needed something that might be used in the gulf and the ocean. Something with two motors, a cabana top, and two swivel seats in the aft and front of the boat."

"Do you have a price range?" the salesman asked.

"How much would a Sea Hunt with two engines cost." Said Ed'

"We have 2 of them inside. Let's go in and look at them." They went inside to look at the two boats.

"This one is 25 feet with the Bimini sun cover and two four-stroke Yamaha 250s on it." Said the salesman. "It's a great all-around boat. It will handle eight persons."

"What's the price of it with suitable instruments, a depth finder, and a good radio? Said Ed. "Oh, I need two fishing seats, one in front and one in the aft of the boat."

"I will have to work that out for you; while I am doing that, go over and look at 26-footer. It won't take me long. I'm Mel." He left.

They went over to look at the other boat. They got into the boat and sat side by side at the steering wheel.

Ed put his arm around Cindy and held her close. "You like either of these?"

She smiled at him and said the other is a more excellent boat, but can you afford to buy it and the beach house?"

"I can," he replied.

Mell came back with the numbers. "This is what that boat will cost you. He gave the sheet to Ed. We would throw in the GPS and radar."

Ed looked at the paper, and he and Cindy went over and sat in the other boat. "I like this one. "How about the warranty?" he asked Mell.

"It comes with a 2-year factory warranty on everything, and we will extend the warranty for another two years. We will also give you two years' oil changes and inspections," said Mell.

"Write that up for me and give a copy to take home and think about it. I will let you know in two days." Said Ed.

"I Will be right back," said Mell. He left.

Cindy and Ed sat in the console set next to each other till Mell came back. They got out, and Ed took the paper, shook Mells's hand, and left with Cindy.

They drove back to the beach house and sat down. Ed looked at Cindy, "You want a glass of wine."

"Sure," said Cindy.

Ed poured them both a glass of wine, and they sat there looking at the picture of the boat and everything in it. "It looks nice; I think I'm going to buy it," said Ed.

"We missed lunch. I'll fix some supper for us. How about burgers on the grill and a salad." Said Ed.

"That'll be good. I'll fix the salad while you are fixing the burgers." Said Cindy.

They sat there eating the burgers, looking at each other. "I hate to see you leave in the morning." Said Ed.

"I know I feel the same way, but I need to." Said Cindy.

They finished supper and cleaned up. "I'm going to bed as I get up early in the morning." Said Cindy.

Ed looked at her, went to her, and hugged her. He looked into her eyes, said, "You have beautiful eyes," and squeezed her hard.

"Good night," said Cindy and went to her bedroom.

Ed went to bed also. It had been a good day he was thinking.

The next morning, Ed got up and went to the living room. Cindy was standing there with her suitcase.

"You want some breakfast before you leave." Asked Ed.

"No thanks, and I hope it will not be long before I can return." She spoke.

Ed went over and hugged her as she picked up her suitcase. They hugged for a long time, she headed for the door with tears in her eyes. They each looked at each other and whispered goodbye. She was gone and Ed got a cup of coffee and went to the deck feeling sad.

Ed decided to go over and check out his beach house today. He went and got dressed. He left and went to the cafe for some breakfast. He ordered bacon and eggs this morning. He sat there thinking about Cindy, hoping things were ok with him and Cindy.

After his breakfast, he drove to his beach house and went inside. The carpenter was still working even though it was Sunday.

Bud said, "I have finished your shower. Go in and check it out."

"Great," said Ed. He went in and looked the shower all over. Fantastic, he thought.

"Well done," he told Bud.

"Thanks," Bud replied. I will tear out the old countertops today before the granite men arrive tomorrow. It won't take me long as this is just cheap stuff."

"Good," said Ed. He went out to the deck, sat down, and watched the waves. I love this Place, he thought.

His phone rang, it was Joe. "Hello said Ed.

"Hi, Ed just reminding you of our upcoming fishing trip.

"I'll be there," said Ed.

"Just checking, you don't have to bring anything," said Joe and hung up.

Ed got up, went back inside, and looked at the lift. It looked almost done. It will make it much easier than carrying things up and down the stairs He left and got into his car.

He drove out to the executive airport there in Destin. It was large enough for small jets to come in and out. He went into the small building that was the office. A lady was sitting there.

"What kind of planes do you have to rent here," Ed asked her.

"We have several, they are in the hangar. We have Cessna 152, 172, and 182. We have twin Cessna 210 also. We do offer trips with our pilot in our small 6-passenger private jet.

"I'm a flight instructor in all of those except your jet. I will come out later this week and your instructor can check me out in your 182. Ok."

"That will be fine. Just call us; here's our card so the instructor can be here when you come in.

Ed took the card and left. He went back to Bill's beach house and made himself a sandwich. He grabbed a beer from the fridge, sat down on the couch, and turned on a football game. Alabama was playing LSU. He finished his sandwich, stretched out on the couch watched the game, and eventually fell asleep.

It was 4:30 when he woke up. He picked up his iPad and googled the Elks in Destin. He found their website and looked at their schedule of events and food. He was a member of the Elks back home. It looks like they are having rib-eye steaks tonight and music at 6. I think I go see what the pace is like,

He went to his car, drove to the Elks, and entered. They checked his Elk ID on entry. He sat down at the bar. There was a line at a window where you place your Order. He asked the bartender for a Busch long-neck beer. He got up and went to a table, set his beer down, and then went to the window. The lady asked him what he wanted.

"I would like the rib eye medium". He told the lady.

It comes with a baked potato and a salad. The salad bar is right around the corner. That will be $12," she said and handed him a ticket.

"Thanks," said Ed as he paid her.

He went to the salad bar, fixed his salad, and sat at his table. He ate his salad and soon someone called his number. He went to the side window, picked up his steak, and sat back down at his table.

"He looked around at the inside and thought this is a nice large Elks. There were several people there already, and more were coming in. He ate his steak and enjoyed it. The couple who was to perform started playing.

He sat back and thought the music sounded really good. They were playing oldies. The guy was a good singer while playing the keyboard. He went to the bar, got another beer, and returned to his table.

The place filled up. Just then two ladies came over and asked if they could join him as there were no more seats.

"Sure, have a seat," he told them.

They sat down as they had already ordered their dinner. They had ordered shrimp and martinis when they came in.

The waiter brought over a salad and drinks for each of them. They took their salad and began eating it while looking at Ed.

One of the ladies asked Ed, "What is your name? I'm Kelly, and This is Rose."

"I'm Ed "Glad to meet you." Said Ed.

"Where you from?" said Rose.

"I'm from Indiana, down here for a few weeks." Said Ed. Not giving away that he is here longer.

"Do you ladies live here.' Said Ed.

"No, we are from Arkansas, down here for a couple of weeks we go home next week." Said Kelly.

They finished their dinners, and Kelly said, "This is great music, better than our Elks back home."

Ed looked at the ladies and thought they were not bad-looking Southern ladies. He finished drinking his beer and thought about getting another.

"Rose looked at Ed and asked him, "Do you dance?"

"I do sometimes, but I need to go soon." Said Ed.

"Well, you must have time for one dance." Asked Rose.

Ed thought for a moment, looking at her she was a pretty blond. "OK, one dance since it's a slow dance that I like."

They got up and went to the dance floor several couples were out there. He put his arm around her and led her in a slow two-step.

"Wow, you are a really good dancer." She put her head on his shoulder and snuggled close.

Ed thought this is nice but I need to go before something happens. The music stopped and they went back to the table. I love this place thought Ed.

Ed looked at the ladies and said, "I must be going. But I have enjoyed meeting you ladies. Enjoy the evening."

Ed said goodbye to the ladies and they said goodbye to Ed also.

"Wish you could stay said Rose.

Ed smiled and left the building thinking a man could get into trouble down here. I hope I don't run into those ladies again. He drove back to Bill's beach house. Went in and crashed. I love this Place.

The next morning, he got up wondering what Cindy was doing. He got his coffee and went to the deck when his phone rang. It was Cindy.

"Hello Cindy, you get home safe and sound," said Ed.

"Yes, I did. I am going to work with my mother again today with my sister and discuss what to do about the shop in the event we want to sell it." She said on the phone.

"Take your time and work things out carefully, we have plenty of time," Ed said.

"I miss you," said Cindy.

"I do you too." Said Ed.

"What are you going to do today?" asked Cindy.

"Well, I'm going to find a painter and go see how the workers are doing." Said Ed.

"Pick out a good painter," said Cindy.

"That I will do," said Ed.

They hung up. Ed finished his coffee and went inside to call Anne about a painter.

Ed dialed Anne's number.

"Hello," said Anne "How can I help you, Ed."

"I need an individual who does interior painting." Said, Ed.

"Just give me a second here, and I will give you a name and number," she answered.

After a few seconds, she came back with a name.

"Call this lady, she will do a good job and is reasonable." Said Anne.

"Ed waited a few seconds and Anne came back on.

"Her name was Donna," said Ann.

"Thanks," said Ed and hung up and called her right away.

"Hello," said Donna.

"Donna, my name is Ed, and I need a good painter for the house I just purchased." Said, Ed

"Ok, where is it, and when can I meet you," said Donna.

Ed gave her the address and said, "How about today."

"I can meet you there at 10:00 today." She spoke.

"Good see you then." Said Ed. And hung up.

Ed went down to the diner and had his breakfast. After breakfast, he headed to his beach house and waited for the painter.

He heard a truck drive up. The lift man came in and said we have your lift finished. Could you try it out for me? He gave Ed the instructions, and Ed went to the lift and pressed down, and it went down to the area under the house. He got out and shut the door and looked at it. This is going to work out well he thought.

He opened the door, shut it, and pushed up, and the lift went back to his living room. He opened the door and got out.

"This works great." Said Ed.

He gave Red the check for the work.

"Thanks," said Red.

Red left and Ed was really happy with the lift. He heard a car pull up. Must be the painter Ed thought. It   was "Hello she said, "You must be Ed."

"That's me," Ed said "You must be Donna.

"Glad to meet you, Ed," Donna said.

Ed took her through the house and explained what colors went where.

"When can you start" asked Ed.

"I can start this afternoon; I have a helper, and she will be here then with me if that is all right. It will take us three days to finish all of it and will cost you $850.00," she replied.

"Good, go ahead and start, just be careful around Bud working in the kitchen." Said, Ed.

The painter left and Bud came in with the granite man. A large truck also pulled up with the granite tops.

"We're going to get the granite tops put in today, and the Plumber will be here tomorrow to install the new sink," said Bud.

"Good deal," said Ed.

Ed said, "I'll come in later today and see how things are going." Said, Ed.

He left and went back to Bill's beach house.

His phone rang, and it was Cindy, and she was crying.

Hello "Cindy, what's the matter?"

"It's Dave, my Ex-boyfriend. He will not leave me alone. "He even accused me of seeing other men, which is not true. I have friends over several times to get together. I've told him many times it's over and to leave me alone. He doesn't want me to see my friends. He kept calling me last night. I finally turned my phone off. I don't know what to do." Said Cindy.

"I do," said Ed. Pack your bags and come on down for a week or more. Maybe then he will get the idea."

"Ok, I'll call my sister and explain what's going on, and maybe I can get away," Cindy said. She stopped crying.

"Great, let me know. I will be on a fishing trip tomorrow and will not be back until late afternoon. Come on in the house if you beat me here," said Ed.

"I, I, (pause) really appreciate you, Ed. Hope to see you soon." She said and hung up.

Ed hung up and went and sat down to think things over. I think we are going to have a problem here, though. Ex-boys or girlfriends are always around and keep coming back.

It was getting late in the afternoon, and he had not eaten lunch. He decided to go to the officer's club and grab a bite.

He got back around 7 and decided to go to bed early as he had to be at the marina by 6:30 and he was tired. He brushed his teeth, took a shower, and dressed for bed.

The next morning, he arrived at the marina at 6:30, and the guys were already there. It looked like it was going to be a great day. He climbed into the boat with the guys, carrying his water and snacks.

"Good to see you guys again. Said, Ed.

The boat headed out for a 4-hour trip. The men sat and talked about fishing while the captain was going over the safety items, such as baiting your hook and removing the fish.

They arrived at their first fishing spot after about 45 minutes. The Capt. announced drop your lines to 40 feet. They all did and it wasn't long before Ed and Joe hung a large enough red snappers. The deckhand took the fish off the hooks and threw the fish in the cooler.

The others also caught fish. They each had 2. The captain blew the horn to bring them up, yelling over the PA system.

They drove for another 3 minutes, and the Capt. blew the horn and yelled to drop them 30 feet. They all did and started catching fish right away.

"OK, guys, bring them in. You have your limit of red snapper; we're going in. The guys brought their lines in, went into the cabin, and sat down. They each had a beer and talked about how big the fish were.

"We're going to take our fish back to the Officers Club and eat them tonight. You want to join us." Said Joe.

"I sure do. Can I bring Cindy? "Said Ed"

"You bet we would be glad to have her we might bring out significant others also. Said Phil.

The boat arrived at the pier, and the men got off. They watched the fish being cleaned and put in a iced bag. Joe put them in a cooler.

They each tipped the deckhand. They went to their cars.

"Joe said "Will 7:00 be ok with everyone?

"That will be fine," the others said.

Ed said, "See you tonight," and drove to his new beach house. He parked and went inside. He saw the carpenter gone and finished while the painter was still working.

He went in to see how she was doing. She had a helper with her.

"We will have this all done by tonight." She spoke.

Great" said Ed.

Ed left and went back to Bill's beach house. He was tired. He made a sandwich, grabbed a beer, went to the deck, and sat down. It was only 1:00.

His phone rang it was Cindy.

"Hello, Cindy where are you." He answered the phone.

"I'm past Montgomery about 3 ½ hours out." She spoke.

"Good. You will have some time to rest, and we could talk before going out to dinner." Said Ed.

"Good," she hung up.

Ed finished his lunch and beer and went inside to clean up and rest for a while.

Back at Cindy's home, Cindy's ex-boyfriend went into Cindy's bookstore and found out where Cindy had disappeared. He was heading out to find her. That is going to be a problem for Cindy and Ed.

Ed went and sat down and watched some TV while waiting on Cindy. He dozed off when he heard her car pull up. He went to the porch, met her, and hugged her.

"So glad to be here," she said.

Ed carried her suitcase into the spare bedroom. Cindy sat down, took a deep breath, and smiled at Ed.

"Relax now and tell me what is going on with everything." Said Ed.

"Well," said Cindy, "about 2 months ago, Dave and I had a bad break up. He accused me of seeing others and I wasn't as I have many friends in my home town. It got so bad that I could not take it anymore. I finally told him to stay away from me. He began calling and begging me to come back. He has become an angry person."

"Why haven't you told me any of this before now." Said Ed.

"I thought it would just go away, but he has continued to harass me. I can't stop him." Said Cindy.

"Well, you are safe here with me now. We should get you a new phone tomorrow. Let's take the battery out of your phone now, call your sister, and tell her to call me if she needs to talk with you." Said Ed.

"Good idea," said Cindy. She called her sister, gave her Ed's phone number, and gave her phone to Ed to remove the battery.

"We have found an assisted living home for my mother, and my sister will buy half of the shop and business when I am ready. Said Cindy.

"That is fantastic," said Ed. "it's getting late and we are going to the base officers club for dinner with my friends."

"Okay, let me go clean up a bit," Cindy said. She went into her room and returned a few minutes later looking nice, Ed thought.

"They left and drove over to the club on the base where his friends were inside waiting for him. Ed and Cindy approached them where they were seated. Joe stood up and shook Ed's Hand.

"Good to see you and Cindy again. Cindy, this is my wife Pam, Phil's wife Sue, and Fred's wife Jill."

The ladies all acknowledged Cindy. Ed and Cindy sat down at the table.

"I'm glad to meet you all," said Cindy.

The Waiter came over and took everyone's drinks. The men all drank beer, and the ladies drank wine.

The waiter left, and Ed introduced the ladies to Cindy. Then they all began talking to Cindy. They ask her where she is from, how she met Ed, and how long she will be in town.

"Joe asked Ed, "Did you get closed on your beach house, and when do you move in."

"I closed on it Wednesday, and I'll move in early next week. I have everything done except the painting, which will be done tomorrow." Said Ed.

"Good," said Joe, "when can we all come over for a cookout."

"Real soon," said Ed.

The waiter brought over the drinks. He said the fish you brought us will soon be ready.

"Hey Ed, we might go on a yellowfin tuna fishing trip in two weeks. Would you be interested? We will leave on a Tuesday, fish on Wednesday, and come home on Thursday. It will cost each of us $200," said Phil.

"I definitely would. Let me know the dates, and I'll go." Said Ed.

"Maybe us girls can plan a shopping trip for those days. How about you, Cindy." Said Pam.

"I would like to, but it depends on the situation back home. I will have to let you know," Cindy said.

Their food arrived and they continued talking while eating the fish. Ed ordered another round of drinks.

After they had finished eating, they all got up to leave, and Joe said, "We need to do this again."

"Yes," everyone said.

Ed and Cindy left the club, drove back to Bills Beach house, and parked. They went inside without noticing a car parked across the street watching the house. It was Cindy's ex.

Ed and Cindy crashed on the couch for a while. Cindy called her sister to see how things were going back home. After she hung up, she turned to Ed.

"Everything is going well back home, and my sister has hired another lady to help with the bookstore." Said Cindy.

"Good, now you can relax for a while. We will go to my beach house tomorrow and pay the painters as they will be almost finished and we can move in tomorrow afternoon." Said Ed.

"That will be nice, won't it, having your place." Said Cindy

"It will. I have your room for you as the home has two master suites." Said Ed.

"It's getting late. Let's hit the sack." Said Ed.

They both went to their separate bedrooms after hugging each other good night.

The following day, Cindy got up first, made herself a cup of coffee, went to the deck, sat, and watched the waves. She sat there for a while, smiling, feeling good.

She did not notice a man walking down the beach with his hood up, looking up at Cindy.

Ed came out with his cup of coffee.

"Did you sleep well?" He asked Cindy.

"I did." Replied Cindy.

They sat there a while, drinking their coffee.

"You want to go out for breakfast, or you want me to make us some bacon and pancakes." Asked Ed.

"Pancakes and bacon will be fine with me." Said Cindy.

"Okay, let's go in. You set the table, and I will make our breakfast," said Ed.

They went in and Ed got the things out to fix bacon and pancakes while Cindy made the table.

It was not long before Ed was done cooking, and they sat down and enjoyed breakfast together.

"This is nice." Said Cindy.

"It is. I enjoy cooking and eating with you." Said Ed.

After they finished their breakfast, they cleaned up the kitchen and went to their bedrooms to clean up for the day.

They each came out ready for the day.

"Let's go on down to my beach house and see the painters," said Ed

They headed down to Ed's beach house and parked underneath it. The painters were already there. They went up inside and looked at the paint job.

Donna asked, "What do you think of it."

Ed and Cindy walked into every room, looking at the paint job.

"What do you think of it?" Ed asked Cindy.

"I think it is a great job. It looks good." Said Cindy.

"Good," said Ed as he handed Donna a check for her work. "Thanks," he said.

The painters left, and Cindy and Ed sat down out on the deck.

"Let's return to Bill's Beach house, get our stuff, bring it back here, and settle in. I have boxes for the food. We can use the lift to bring it all up." Said Ed.

"Ok," said Cindy.

They went over to the lift, fit in easily, and pressed down. It went down where they got out and went to Ed's car. Cindy noticed a red sedan across the street that looked familiar. She couldn't tell who was inside it. She stared at it as it drove away. She noticed the Tennessee plates and started to shake.

Bill saw her shaking and looking sick. He ran over to her and asked her what was wrong.

"I saw my ex-Dave parked across the street. He drove off when I saw him. What am I going to do." She asked Ed.

"I don't know right now, but we will figure something out. Ier's get in the car.

They drove back to Bill's beach house and went in. Ed sat down with Cindy and consoled her, and she settled down.

"He can not hurt you in any way as long as you are with me. I will make some plans to deal with him. Now, let's get packed and move into my beach house.

They began packing everything up, including some groceries. And I loaded it all into Ed's car.

Ed was on the lookout for Dave's car and was making plans. Ed locked up Bill's house and they drove over to his beach house. They used the lift to put everything up inside the house. They put everything away as they were quiet, thinking about what was next.

I'll fix us a couple of drinks, and we can sit on the deck and watch the waves come in. It puts the mind at ease. Cindy went out to the decks and sat down while Ed fixed their drinks so they were not too strong.

He went out, handed Cindy her drink, and sat down. He smiled at Cindy.

"Thanks, Ed." She said, sipping on the drink.

"You are welcome," said Ed, "Toast'"

They touched their glasses together. They sat there for a while relaxing.

"How would you like to go on a cruise to the eastern Caribbean." Said Ed. "We could catch a cruise out of Florida."

"Oh, I would love to as soon as I finish resolving my problems at home." Replied Cindy.

"I think I'll take a walk on the beach," said Cindy

"OK, I'll sit here and enjoy the view." Said Ed.

Cindy went down the steps to the beach and walked east slowly, looking at the shells. She was carrying her shoes so she could walk in the low waves.

She had walked for about six minutes when she looked up, and Dave appeared before her. This scared her, and she screamed loudly.

"Get away from me she yelled at him."

He moved back from her. People were looking at them.

People were gathering around. Dave tried to touch her and she jerked away.

"Don't touch me!" yelled Cindy. She moves back away from him.

"I still want to be with you. Why don't you like me," Dave said.

"I don't like you, and I don't want to be around you. Leave me alone," she yelled. Get away from me."

"Someone please call the police," she told the crowd. They did.

Ed heard the screaming and yelling and saw the crowd. He jumped up and down to the beach and ran down and saw it was Cindy yelling at a man.

He ran up, grabbed the man by his collar, and lifted him up. Ed was considerably larger than the man. Ed realized it was Dave, the man who was stalking Cindy.

"Don't you ever come near Cindy again, or you will have to answer to me," said Ed. He shoved Dave and started to run.

Just then, the police arrived. Cindy told the police what had happened. The police grabbed Dave and held onto him.

The police listened to Cindy's story of Dave stalking her and following her down here.

"Do you want us to arrest him or just hold him for a while until you come down and fill out a restraining order on him?" Said the policeman.

Cindy looked at Ed.

"Do it," said Ed. "That will resolve your problem with him. I don't think he will bother you again." Said, Ed.

The police left with Dave and the crowd dispersed. Ed and Cindy walked back to the beach house with Ed's arm around Cindy.

They got to the beach house and went up and sat down. They finished their drink.

"It was getting late and Ed said let's go down to the cafe and get something to eat." Said, Ed

They went and took the lift down, got in Ed's car, and drove to the cafe. They went in and sat down.

Ed reached over, took Cindy's hand, and said, "Things are going to work out.

"I know they will, and I feel better now since he's probably out of my life for good." Said Cindy.

The waiter came over, and they both ordered iced tea.

"I think I am going to order half order of Rockefeller oysters," said Ed.

"Oh, I like those." Said Cindy.

"Good, then I'll order a full order of one dozen, and we can spit the order." Said, Ed.

The waiter came with their drinks and they placed their whole order of oysters.

"I need to go back home and temporarily resolve things there. If I can get things done there, I will come back down, and we can do some serious talking," Cindy said.

"That works for me." Said, Ed.

The oysters arrived, smiled at each other, and enjoyed their meal together. After dinner, they left, returned to the beach house, and sat on the couch watching a movie. They got tired and went to their bedrooms for the night.

The following day, Cindy came out, and Ed had pancakes ready. Ed poured Cindy a cup of coffee.

"These are good pancakes, Ed.," said Cindy.

"Thank you. Let's go down to the police station and get your restraining order in place so you can relax.

"Ok," said Cindy

They finished the pancakes and went to the police station, where Cindy completed all the paperwork.

"That was easy." Said Cindy.

They left the police station, and Ed said, "I want to take you to the Navy Museum today. I think you would enjoy that.

"Let's go, that sounds interesting," said Cindy.

They got into the car and headed west for about an hour and a half. They parked and went into the extensive museum, which was full of naval airplanes.

"Wow said Cindy." This is neat.

They walked around, and Ed told her about some of the planes. They got to the F4 Phantom. I loved flying a plane like this. It's a great plane. The day I retired, I ejected from one like this. I came out ok.

"It looks like a monster to fly. It looks mean." Cindy said.

"It was a mean machine during its time." Said, Ed.

They walked around for another hour, and Cindy said, "I'm tired. Could we go?"

"Ok," said Ed, and they headed back to the car and drove back to the beach house.

When they got there, They took the lift up. They sat down on the couch. Cindy looked at Ed and said, "I'm going back home in the morning.

"I figured you would be leaving." Said Ed.

It's getting late. I'm going to make us some sandwiches He made the sandwiches and poured some iced tea. Let's go to the deck and sit for a while and enjoy ourselves."

"Ok," said Cindy.

"I'm feeling a lot better since the ordeal with my ex is over," said Cindy.

"Good," said Ed; after they finished eating, they went inside. "I'm going to bed as I'm getting up early to leave," said Cindy.

Ed went over and hugged her. "Good night, sleep tight."

They each went to bed for the night. Ed went to sleep thinking about Cindy.

Ed got up the next morning, and Cindy was standing in the middle of the living room with a cup of coffee and her bags at her side. "Im heading out" she said and I thank you for everything. I'll call you soon."

Ed hugged her goodbye. "You drive safe, and I will be thinking about you." He took her coffee cup and she took the lift down to her car and drove off.

Ed poured himself a cup of coffee and went to the deck. He sat there for a while, watching some dolphins play in the gulf.

Cindy called while he was sitting there and told Ed she would be gone for a week or more.

"You take care of things. I gave you a key to my beach house in case you can come down while I am gone.

The guys and I are going on a fishing trip in about three days and will be gone for three or four days. You take care." Ed hung up.

The next few days, Ed hung around his beach house, straightening things up and cleaning up around the outside of the house.

His phone rang and it was Joe. "Ed, "We will be by there to pick you up at 08:30 in the morning.

"I'll be ready. "Said Ed.

"Great. "Said Joe and hung up

Ed went into the house and grabbed a bite to eat. It was getting dark, and Ed thought I had better get some rest before tomorrow morning.

Early the following morning he headed for the marina. His friends were right on time. Ed had packed a small travel bag of snacks and fishing clothes. He took the lift down. They were waiting under his house for them. He climbed into the back seat after putting his bag in the trunk.

Sit back and relaxed. It's about 4.5 hours before we arrive at the marina in Venice, Louisiana, and check in with the Capt. of the boat that we will be on. We will have to buy our state fishing licenses when we get there. We have reservations at a small cottage there.

They headed west on I-10. They drove for about 2 hours, pulled off the interstate, and parked at a small restaurant for breakfast. They went in and sat down.

Ed said, "I want some coffee and biscuits and gravy."

"That sounds good," said Bill.

The rest ordered the same. They finished their breakfast and headed on down I-10. They went through the tunnel at Mobile and entered Mississippi. They arrived at the marina in Louisiana around 3 PM.

After they checked in with the boat and got their fishing licenses, they went to the motel.

"There is a nice place around the corner. It's called Dan's Lounge." Said Phil.

"Let's go. I'm hungry." Said Fred.

They all ordered a beer and talked about fishing tomorrow.

"We'll have a good time tomorrow. I have some bromine that we all should take two hours before we go out," said Phil.

The waiter came back over and took their order of burgers and fries. After they finished eating, they went back to the two rooms they had at the cottage and crashed for the night.

The following day, they drove over to the marina, found their boat, The Lazy Bone, and climbed aboard. Captain Ron welcomed them aboard and introduced them to the deckmate, James.

They all shook his hand. James took them around the boat and explained everything to them, including safety items and how to use the poles. We were going out about 40 miles to a place called Midnight Gap. Find a place to relax as it will take about 2 ½ hours to get there.

We will fish for about 3 to 4 hours before heading back. Hopefully, we will have at least four tuna fish for you guys. There is a chance of storms out there after 4:30 today, but we want to beat them back before then.

They found places to relax on the boat, which had provisions in case they were hungry or thirsty.

The ride seemed smooth enough, but there were not really large waves. The boat did heave up a couple of times with the waves but posed no problems for the guys.

They arrived at the fishing site, and the captain announced to get the poles ready and drop to about 300 feet. The deckhand came by each person and baited their hooks with live Herring. They dropped their lines to about 300 feet.

They waited, watching other boats out there, and once in a while, they would hear someone yell fish on. They looked at the boat and watched the fisherman on the other boat pull in a nice fish.

Just then Phil's pole jumped and was bending over. You got one." Yelled James.

Phil was fighting the fish, walking back and forth along the back and reeling in hard. Everyone else had brought their lines in. After about 45 minutes, it got up where they could see it, and James gaffed it and brought it into the boat.

Nice tuna said, James. It looks about 7 lbs and large enough to keep. He put the fish into the ice bin. They all dropped their lines again and waited.

Ed was the next one to catch one and it went into the cooler. Phil hung another and fought it until it got off the hook.

After a few minutes, Phil's pole bent over again, and he grabbed it, and Joe yelled I got one on, too. They fought their fish for several minutes before Phils came up close enough to bring it in.

It took Joe another 15 minutes before he could get his in. All 4 fish were in the cooler and the guys were really happy looking at the fish.

Just Then, the Capt. announced to them that they were going in because it looked like a storm way out west. "You men enter the cab and brace yourself for large waves in about ½ hour."

All the lines were in and secured. They went in and found a good place to sit. The captain came down to the cabin to drive from there toward the shore.

The going was okay for about ½ hours, and they still had about 2 hours to go. The clouds started to come in, and the waves became more significant. The boat was heaving up and down and side to side.

"Everyone put the life jackets on." Yelled the Capt.

They put on their jackets. The waves were growing more extensive, and just then, the cabin door flew open. Phil jumped up to close it as the boat leaned sideways again, and Phil went flying, hitting his head on the chair handle and falling.

Ed grabbed him and lifted him to a bench and the other held him. Just then, Ed fell to the floor and hurt his arm and leg badly. James helped him up to a bench. Ed held on to a post by his seat to keep from falling off again.

The weather was getting a lot worse. The Capt. I called the Coast Guard on the emergency line: "Coast Guard, this is The Lazy Bone at Lat N29.25 and W 93.17 declaring an emergency."

"What is the emergency?" replied the Coast Guard.

"We have two injured men on board and four others onboard. We are in severe weather and have a chance of capsizing." The Capt. Told the Coast Guard.

"We think we have you on our radar, and a team will depart ASAP. It looks like the worst weather will clear up for you soon, maybe ¾ hours. Hang on. We are about an hour or more out," said the Coast Guard.

Just then, a huge wave hit the boat. It turned over to its side and rolled almost entirely on its side. The men all fell to the floor hard. The boat had filled up with a lot of water. Then the boat rolled back upright, and the men got back up to their seats and found bars to hang on to. They held on to help Phil as he was starting to wake up.

Just then, the boat's bow heaved way up, and the men started to rise up as the boat slammed down hard, and the men hit their seats hard.

The men yelled out, everyone held on tight, and they were all hurting as the storm kept on hammering the boat.

Just then, the boat's radio came on, and one of the other boats called out on the radio that they were sinking and needed help. The Capt yells at the men, "Our Bildge pump is pimping out the water. It looks like we will be fine. Just hold on.

The captain kept on fighting the storm, and soon, the rain quit, and the wind died down a little as the storm started passing. The guys were starting to breathe easier. The captain said, "We are still about three hours out from the marina." The weather is still really rough, so hold on for a while longer.

James looked at Phil and he was coming around. "You just hang on. We have help coming real soon."

"Phil smiled and relaxed. James went over and looked at Ed's arm. "It looks like you have broken it below the elbow," said James.

Just then, they heard the helicopter over them. The Capt. stopped the boat. The helicopter had opened its door.

The men had come out as a Coast Guard man came down on a sling and gurney. They got Phil onto the sling, and he was raised up. The waves kept moving the boat around and the sling. The next sling came down, and Ed got in, and he was raised up.

Joe and Fred waved goodbye to their friend. And the Copter was turning to leave when they yelled over a megaphone if they could make it back to shore. The Capt. Yelled back, "Yes."

The Copter left, and the boat headed back to the marina. It took them another 1 ½ hours before they got to the dock. The waves hammered the boat all the way back until the boat entered the safe area of the marina.

Joe and Fred got off the boat and sat at a bench nearby while watching the deckhand clean their tuna. They were exhausted and a little bruised up.

The deckhand cleaned their fish, put them into their cooler, iced it down, and shut it up.

"That should last at least 3 hours before you get home," said James.

"Thanks," said Joe and tipped him well.

They loaded it into their SUV and got in, and they looked at each other.

"You think we can return home without stopping? They were still hurting, maybe switching drivers halfway," Said Joe.

"Yes, I do." Said Fred.

They head back up to l-10 and home.

On the way back, Joe received a call from Capt., Who Said Ed and Phil were in the USA hospital in Mobile, Alabama.

"Ok, thanks." Said Joe. He passed it on to Fred.

Fred said, "Let's get this fish home, and in the morning, we will head over to see them."

"Good Idea." Said Joe.

They continued driving and Fred took a short nap and woke up after about an hour. "I can drive now until we get home," said Fred.

Joe pulled over at the Alabama rest area and switched drivers after a restroom stop. Fred drove the rest of the way home.

They arrived at Joe's home and put the fish in the freezer. Joe drove Fred over to his house. And went back home. Joe was tired and went to bed. It was 9 PM.   Joe woke the next morning refreshed, and his phone rang. It was Ed. "Hello Ed, you ok." Said, Joe

"Yes, and so is Phil. We just need a ride home," said Ed. The food is great, and the nurses are great. They are treating us very well."

"We'll be there at 1:00 to get you. Will that work? Replied Joe.

"We'll be ready." Said Ed and hung up.

Back in Tennessee, Cindy was watching the news. The news talked about 3 fishing boats off of the Louisiana coast being in trouble. They were caught off guard by a big storm that popped up. One boat sank, and the other two barely made it back to shore. Two fishermen were rescued by the Coast Guard and taken to the hospital in Mobile with injuries.

Cindy panicked and tried calling Ed, but there was no answer. She paces back and forth, watching the news. She then tried Joe as Ed had given her his phone number. She dialed his number.

"Hello," said Joe.

"Joe, this is Cindy. Where is Ed, and is he okay?" Replied Cindy and she began crying.

"Easy," said Joe. "He is in the hospital in Mobile, Al. He has a broken arm and a bruised leg. We are going over to get him soon and bring him and Phil back home. He is all right. Don't you worry? He is being well taken care of.

"I'm coming down tomorrow to see him, and I can care for him. Don't tell him, as he has enough problems." Said Cindy.

"That will be fine. He will be pleased to see you. We were through a hell of a storm. It was terrible out there. You drive carefully. Joe said, "Everything will be alright," and he hung up the phone.

Joe and Fred headed out down I-10 to Mobile USA Hospital. He arrived at 12:30, went into the hospital, and asked the receptionist where Ed Martin's room was. She told him, and he went up to Ed's room. Phil was in the next room.

The nurses were getting them ready to leave. Joe hugged them and looked them over.

"You guys look fine. The nurses laughed and said, "They have been great patients."

Ed and Phil laughed, saying, "The food is great, and we have been treated great. "Let's go home."

They were wheeled down to the SUV in wheelchairs, laughing about their ordeal even though it was terrifying at times. They got into the SUV independently and "yelled home, Joe."

"Ed said, "I think I am going to write a book about this adventure he laughed."

They arrived at Ed's beach house first. "You need help?" asked Joe.

"Nope, I'm fine. Thanks for the ride home. He limped to his lift and went up to his living room. He went into the bathroom and took a long hot shower. It felt great. I think I will go to the base officer's club and have a beer and something to eat.

When he arrived, the guys were all there, and everyone was congratulating them on getting home safely. Joe explained their ordeal in the storm and the help from the Coast Guard helicopter. The crowd was all ears.

They saw Ed walk in and cheered him. He limped over with his arm in a sling, and they pulled up a chair for him. They all patted him on the back, careful not to hit his arm.

"I'm hungry" and need a beer. Said Ed.

"One beer coming up, and the house special is tacos, and they are on the house for you guys. He yelled to the bartender, "Taco's please."

"You guys have been all over the news. Glad your home is safe," said the waiter.

They all enjoyed the evening, and it started getting late. They headed home really happy.

Ed got home and crashed for the evening. It was 8:00 when he got up the next morning. He grabbed a cup of coffee, sat down on the couch, and watched the news on TV. The men were on the news again.

He finished his coffee, went in, took a long hot shower, got dressed, and then went into the kitchen and thought about breakfast. I think I'll get a cup of coffee and sit on the deck for a while.

He walked out on the Deck and looked out at the gulf and down at the beach. He looked closely, and there was Cindy standing on the beach crying, looking up at him.

Ed yelled, "Cindy," and headed down the steps to limping.

Cindy started running, her arm reaching out towards him. They met with their outstretched arms, looked at each other, tears running down her cheeks, and locked themselves in a long, warm kiss.

They pulled apart and Cindy said, "Oh Ed, I love you so much, I was worried I would never see you again." She kissed him again.

Ed pushed her back and said, "I love you more than you know, and I don't want us to leave each other again. They Kissed again.

They went up into the house holding hands and sat down.

"When I saw the story on TV about the boats and storm, it said two men had been injured, and a boat had sunk. I did not know what to do. You never answered your phone. I finally got a hold of Joe and felt much better. I knew then I was deeply in love with you and I had to be with you. I packed up and came down." Cindy said, still crying a little.

Ed gave her a napkin and spoke. Well, when I was lying in the hospital, I knew then I wanted to be with you forever, also.

Ed said, "Let's have a drink and a toast to us, call the guys and their wives over for a cookout, and celebrate our future together.

"Yes," said Cindy; she got up and danced a little happy jig.

Ed clapped and watched her. He thought I love this Place. It's full of beautiful places and people.

THE END

EDDIE ADVENTURE I, II, III, IV, V

Upcoming

ROMANCE AMONG THE PECAN TREES

The author retired from the US Air Force and Purdue University. He has a BS from Purdue University. He traveled from Germany to Alaska. He spent a lot of time with his two boys and his father hunting and fishing in Montana, Alaska, Alabama, Oregon, and many other states. He enjoyed flying as a Flight Instructor. It was a pleasure putting these adventures into books.